To
Gordie +
Thanks for your [...]
and encouragement,
Good neighbors and great
friends.

Larry Hamilton
8/21/09

Lucy's
STORY

Omavi & Asali Publishing
P.O. Box 143
Piqua, OH 45356
www.omaviasalipublishing.com

Book cover layout by Lawrence E. Hamilton Jr., Nikki DeLaet,
Christy Albers, and Nancy Neal

Picture of refugee camp used with permission of University of Kentucky
ID: KUKAV-77PA103-02 "Camp Nelson Photographic Collection, 1864"
University of Kentucky Special Collections

Kentucky Historical Markers used with permission of Dr. Stephen McBride

Illustrations on front cover, chapter pages, and painting on back cover by
Linda S. Hamilton

Graphic designer Nikki DeLaet

ISBN 978-0-9824721-0-1

In Dedication to:

The Author and Finisher of our faith ...

My Best Beloved, who has made this
sojourn a "heaven" on earth.

My parents for their unfailing generosity
and goodness. (Thanks, Dad and Mom,
for the thesaurus!)

My sister whose faithful encouragement
is a bright spot. This would not
have been possible without you.

Mr. Larry Hamilton for affording me the
opportunity to fulfill a dream. Thank you.

Mrs. Barb Davis whose effort and skill
made this work into all it has become.

And to all those "asleep in Jesus"
who have a story to tell.

C.D.

Foreward

For heart of man though mainly right,
Hides many things from mortal sight
Which seldom ever come to light
Except upon compulsion.

Frederick Douglass, "What am I to you"
Submitted by Michael Crutcher who personifies the
"spirit of Douglass" and served
as the president of the Camp Nelson Foundation.

The United States of America had been a nation for nearly 75 years when the plight of the enslaved could no longer be sanctioned as an engine for growth and prosperity in a land that claimed to be a bastion for liberty and freedom. Abraham Lincoln expressed the foreboding storm clouds gathering with his declaration, *"A house divided against itself cannot stand. I believe this government cannot endure permanently half-slave and half-free."*

The Civil War exposed the fallibility of the words the Founding Fathers provided in framing the Constitution, but the conflict would reassert the principle of inalienable rights and lead to the expansion of democratic ideas, now encompassing a class and race previously excluded. Americans had approached this climax knowing that decades of ignorance would reveal a necessity for change and enlightenment. Frederick Douglass captured this sentiment in finding that the hidden dark things of man's heart "must needs be" brought to light by compulsion.

In the nineteenth century, amid the throes of the War Between the States, Camp Nelson was created. Its establishment was situated high above the limestone bluffs of the Kentucky River separating Jessamine and Garrard Counties and about 25 miles south of Lexington. Its origination was for the men of war. It was a chief center designed for the recruiting and preparation of white soldiers, as well as a regional supply base. This amazing military base, known for its modern "technology" of the era and organizational expertise, produced defensive security as well as the ability to launch operations through the Cumberlands into Virginia and Tennessee. Camp Nelson also became a haven for many Kentucky slaves. Slaves fled their masters seeking the protection of sympathetic Union soldiers stationed there and were given the opportunity to remain there as laborers, cooks and washerwomen. Most importantly, the decision to recruit blacks into the union ranks swelled the number of slaves seeking their own personal emancipation along with those who were energized to take up arms for the liberation of their people. They began to serve without the yoke of bondage and be educated for a future in a newly united nation state. Black people began to utilize their gifts and change history forever. Camp Nelson would challenge the superiority mindset of the nineteenth century and test the birth of equality—both physically and spiritually.

The past meshes into the future, which in time becomes our "present." Can we presently question ourselves, in true humility, ensampled by the Most Just, to perceive what hidden ignorance or prejudice we might possess within our inner hearts? In Frederick Douglass' words, we should strive to seek that which is hidden from our mortal sight.

Acknowledgments

Lucy's Story could never have been written without my meeting Alex Haley who inspired the oral history interview of my grandmother, Esther Hannon Hamilton, in November 1975. For many years I subjected my wife, Linda, and children Lawrence, III (Butch), Cicely, Erika and Jonathan to countless hours of listening to family history stories on that tape as we drove in the car to various destinations. I thank them for their tolerance of a husband and father that was often unyielding to other family requests for more conventional listening fare.

From an early age I had an intense interest in studying history and a love for being around a large extended family group of Hamilton and Greene relatives in Loveland, Ohio, for which I can thank my parents Mary F. (Greene) and Lawrence E. Hamilton, Sr. Growing up and going to school in Loveland suited me well with inspirational teachers like Mrs. Hutchinson, who was stern and yet encouraging at the elementary level. Mr. Russell Duncanson gave me the opportunity to shine and display my knowledge of history in junior high. I became the frequent winner of his classroom history game called Line-up, which allowed me to know that I was among the best history students in the school. At the high school my focus shifted to sports more than academics, but a special thanks to Coach Stan McCoy for seeing enough athletic talent in me that an athletic grant-in-aid to Central State University was made possible.

At CSU I truly fell in love with history. I greatly admired the university president, Dr. Charles Wesley, who was a prominent historian. His fraternal scholarship and the urging of my Alpha Phi Alpha Fraternity brothers to excel academically were highly motivational. While at Central, I also had the good fortune to learn that the black man had an illustrious history. I thoroughly enjoyed being taught by Mrs. Wilhelmina 'Ma' Robinson and Dr. Joe Lewis and because of those lessons, I committed myself to becoming a history teacher upon graduating from CSU.

The recruitment to teach a black history course at Piqua High School led me to move to the west central Ohio city where I was given the opportunity to teach that course for thirty consecutive years. At Piqua I was blessed to meet Arthur Thomas who mentored me in the use of genealogical tools and encouraged me in the research of the stories that my grandmother had told. The African American Genealogical Group of the Miami Valley (AAG-GMV) was also helpful in providing the research skills that equipped me to use the resources made available through the assistance of Pat Van Skaik and the staff of the Cincinnati and Hamilton County Public Library. Thanks also to AAGGMV member Bennie McRae, an expert on black soldiers and the United States Colored Troops (USCT's) in the Civil War stationed at Camp Nelson. Thanks to the research of Dr. Richard Sears in his writing of *Camp Nelson, Kentucky*, which was used as a primary reference in the writing of *Lucy's Story*. Archivist Shannon Wilson and the staff at Berea College have always been wonderfully supportive in research visits to the campus. Thanks to Michael Crutcher and the Camp Nelson Foundation for their effort to preserve the history of the camp from the perspective of both the soldiers and the refugees. Special thanks go to Rita Fox from Garrard County, Kentucky, who encouraged me to submit a family history article in her publication *Paint Lick Reflections*, and to Judy Clark Adams who shared her family history research and gave me a tour of the farm where many of my ancestors were enslaved.

As a retired teacher I was given the opportunity by Leesa Baker to make family history presentations at the Piqua YWCA and to make black history offerings through the Piqua Library. I was further supported by the Piqua community in the formation of Promoting Recognition of Diversity (PROD), the passage of a City Resolution based upon the RIGHT Concept and the creation of a taskforce and committee on diversity formed by the City Commission. Both as a colleague at PHS and a personal friend I have long had the support of Barb Davis and her husband, Dale, who have always given me an attentive ear on various ideas and proposals. Since Barb has long had a habit of correcting my test papers and instructive materials on the blackboard at school, I have called upon her once again. Without her assistance in proofreading and offering suggestions to improve the quality of this offering, *Lucy's Story* would not be what it has now become.

Thanks to my dear and loving wife who has made numerous sacrifices to allow me to travel to conduct research and make family history presentations. I thank her, too, for her artistic talent in creating illustrations within the book that enhances the visual effect in reading *Lucy's Story*.

The DeLaet family was instrumental in the publication of this work. Nikki was supportive in her role as an intermediary and her computer expertise and Bob and Diane for consulting on printing matters.

It is not often possible for a teacher to experience the joy of knowing that he has made a difference in the lives of his students but it is nearly impossible to convey the joy and pride that I possess in having a student that has made such a dramatic and life-altering contribution to her teacher's life as Christina DeLaet has by writing the story of my family history. Thank you, Tina. You actually asked for nothing but the opportunity to satisfy my desire in having this story told and written. Thank you, Tina, and thanks to your husband, Mark, and your children for their sacrifices in allowing you to labor through the completion of *Lucy's Story: Right Choices but Wrongs Still Left*.

Finally, I thank GOD for ordering my path from the time of being a student in my grandmother's Sunday School class at the Loveland Predestinarian Baptist Church unto this current time of being a member and Sunday School teacher myself at the Greater Love Missionary Baptist Church.

Introduction

On the 25th anniversary of the television miniseries *Roots: The Saga of an American Family* I wrote a commentary that began:

> Some call it fate. Alex Haley described it as
> "a meant-to-be series of incidents." But, as one who
> was baptized in the Predestinarian Baptist Church in
> Loveland, Ohio (a Cincinnati suburb) I know it to be
> something even deeper, that which was preordained
> and divinely sanctioned.

One of the occurrences in the meant-to-be series of incidents was the choice I made on November 19th of 1975 to take members of my black history class at Piqua High School on a field trip to nearby Wright State University to hear a speaker named Alex Haley. It was indeed a spiritual and transforming experience.

I was awed by Haley's story of a family saga because I too had a grandmother (Esther Hannon Hamilton) who in my youth frequently pumped me full of stories about her grandmother (Lucy Sams). Great-great-grandmother Sams had told Esther about her time at Camp Nelson during or shortly after the conclusion of the Civil War.

So, having had the conversion experience of listening to Alex Haley, that very evening I called my grandmother to make arrangements to come home to Loveland to interview her and record some of the stories I had heard in my youth. The interview for which I was poorly prepared lasted over three hours but I had brought with me only one tape with a recording time of one hour. Having finished making the tape I strangely let it sit in my desk for over twenty years before I realized that it was I who had been anointed to confirm the authenticity, if possible, and to share the family history research with relatives and others.

This effort would eventually become the basis for this book, *Lucy's Story: Right Choices but Wrongs Still Left.*

The final strange occurrence that I attribute to a divinely ordered experience was the arrival of a letter just before February 2008 from a former student who had taken my black history class at Piqua High School. She had read about a series of upcoming Black History Month presentations that I was scheduled to make at Edison Community College in Piqua and the session that had caught her interest the most was Camp Nelson: Black Soldiers and Refugee Slaves. She stated that she would be attending the evening of the Camp Nelson presentation. But because the weather had turned so inclement that night she, along with many others, was unable to attend that activity. That situation prompted a second letter expressing the sorrow of not being able to be there and a question of whether I would be willing to meet with her at her parents shop, Eagle Printing & Graphics, to share with her personally this story of my family's experience at this Civil War camp. I was, of course, delighted to do so. When we met it occurred to me that I had memories of this student because she had been so shy and a little socially withdrawn from her classmates. Nevertheless, she claimed the class had stimulated a profound interest in reading nineteenth century literature, particularly of the slave experience. She added that when she wasn't busy with taking care of her husband and their five children, she liked to dabble in writing stories of that era.

Despite the fact that Christina DeLaet no longer was my student and could now probably demonstrate more knowledge of the slave experience than her former teacher, I nevertheless felt compelled to subject her to an examination. I sent her a test that, unbeknownst to her, would determine whether or not she might be capable of helping me relate the story of my family's historical legacy.

So, like my own college professors of many years back, I composed an essay question. In essence, I threw a blue book at her to see how she would respond to the question I posed--the question I hoped would become the opening story line for a family history novel. With the thought that her response would give me an idea of how she might expand on my story idea, here is the question I put forth:

> She was once young and beautiful but her yellow skin
> had long since lost the luster and brilliance of a golden
> presence in the midst of her darker granddaughters who
> were now bathing her because she was unable to do
> so herself.

Her response to my deceptively probing trial and examination of her literary skills is what has now become the Prologue for this book and prompted the following congratulatory appeal to continue the use of her writing talent in telling the stories garnered from my family history research:

May 9, 2008

Dear Tina,

I am a strong believer in the divine force of predestination. I know that GOD has directed our paths to intersect in spite of our physical journey having begun long ago without the knowledge of one another. We come from different racial, ethnic, cultural and denominational backgrounds but strangely there is a spiritual component that seems to suggest to me that our lives will intertwine in a meaningful way that demonstrates the ability to overcome differences on the part of those who are willing to humble themselves and recognize that humanity is subject to the sovereignty of something greater than ourselves. The point that I am trying to make is that the letter you wrote expressing your desire to come and hear my presentation on Camp Nelson was not solely that of a former student sharing an interest in a subject area relating to a teacher with whom she held fond recollections of classroom experiences some time ago. No! I now realize that it is something potentially greater than that and a part of what I perceive as a meant-to-be collaboration in sharing another piece of the story of the mosaic of the American family. Tina, I have known for some time that I have been called upon to tell the story of my family and even more importantly I recognized that the telling would also be in a written manner in book form. I've never thought of myself as a writer and always knew that someone would be shown to me that would fill the areas of deficiency in my ability to have my family story presented in a descriptive and literary way. Tina, I believe that someone is you. Your old teacher again subjected you to a test and you passed with flying colors. I loved your writing style and your ability to develop a character and describe a setting.

WE NEED TO TALK!
Larry Hamilton

That talk has resulted in the publication of *Lucy's Story...* which is based upon various stories handed down to me by my family—particularly from Lucy Sams, a refugee at Camp Nelson, and Bryant Greene, my great-great-grandfather and a soldier with the Sixth U.S. Colored Cavalry, who was stationed at Camp Nelson. In addition, stories of Clark, Royston and Merritt slave descendants of Garrard County just south of Camp Nelson have been included.

1920

Prologue

It all came down to this. After three score years and more of living, two striplings of granddaughters had relegated her back to her infancy. They ordered her about like they expected she would listen.

"Mammy, you need your bath and we're going to give you one. Jus' you don't worry none," Esther informed her, placing a warm hand on her grandmother's cold shoulder. The other granddaughter, Ethel, clucked in agreement.

Mammy eyed their washing apparatus suspiciously. Esther produced a bucket, Ethel a washbowl. Mammy wasn't too old she couldn't let her mind be known. "I grew up with a wooden bucket in my hand." The girls nodded. "I cleaned and scrubbed and toted water seems nearly all my life in a wooden bucket." Now she had no need for a wooden bucket. Times changed, didn't they?

Esther patted Mammy's swollen fingers and went for a bar of soap. "Bathed and emptied slop out of the same bucket.

Don't 'spect you girls ever had to do that?" Ethel got warm water. "Here, Mammy," Esther coaxed, lathering a clean cloth. Mammy drew back. "You girls ain't washin' me in no ol' wooden bucket!" Her lungs did not suffer from old age as her limbs did.

"Mammy, you have to have a bath. It's for your health. I know you've always done it yourself but—."

"Don't see why I got to be bathed!"

"Mammy, you need—."

"Mammy, we only want to—-."

"Ain't no rest for an old soul. Person gets on in years and everybody thinks they got the right to be bossin' and sassin'—."

"Mammy, you stink!"

Mammy's gray head rotated upward. Her steel gray eyes pinned her granddaughter, full of hurt.

Esther and Ethel knelt by their grandmother's side. Ethel spoke, hoping to ease the sting of the words. "Please, Mammy, we want to help. Let us do this thing for you."

Mammy saw the pleading dark eyes. In times past, how often had she seen dark eyes plead, for forgiveness, for mercy, for love? She grunted, turning away. "Use the washbowl."

In her youth, Mammy had been beautiful. Her skin, a yellow tone like an exotic lily, had once radiated a brilliance begotten of Eve. But oh, beauty skin deep had its own snare. As usual, the past crept forward, its obnoxious tendrils much like a vine that entwined itself around other living things.

Now her golden presence paled under her granddaughters' ministrations. How capable their strong dark hands were! Her luster had faded and melted away beneath the beauty of their rich sable skin. She often lamented her light color. But her desire was fulfilled in watching her granddaughters' dark hands tend to their chore.

Esther stood and tried to remove her grandmother's housedress. Mammy froze her rocker in mid-motion. Fear stole over her mind, blurring the future, fleshing the past. The old woman would disrobe for no one, not even her granddaughters. Mammy struck out awkwardly behind her in an attempt to still the hands intent on their job.

"Mammy—." Esther gave a jerk. The old faded housedress gave way. Esther gasped. Ethel followed Esther's riveted gaze.

The back before them was scarred, a map of contours resembling ridged mountains crisscrossing a small continent. Old corrugated flesh met the girls' eyes. Esther covered her mouth with the back of her hand to still her cry.

Mammy's old eyes, long void of moisture, gave forth several tears. She sighed. It had all come down to this. Shame was a hovering visage again, after all these years. Her two granddaughters fell to their knees before her. Tears rolled down her weathered cheeks. Mammy attempted to swipe at them. Her throaty voice spoke, "Girls, the Bible tells us by His stripes we are healed. Ain't nothin' been healed by mine." She laid her gnarled hands on the troubled youthful cheeks of her granddaughters. "Some things only come to be after much hurt." Yes, of course, it would come to this.

Mammy's mind returned to that which refused to be forgotten. Her eyes stared sightlessly through a multitude of years. "They called me Lucy, there, where I was born, over in Madison County, on the Redmond plantation. It was thereabouts 1845, when the locusts start their hummin'. You girls know that place? Born right on Kentucky dirt. And I mean, right on its dirt ...."

Chapter 1

Madison County 1850 - 1863

Differences

The hills were unfledged and verdant, trees speckling them into the next county. In the beginning, Lucy had gazed at them from the cabin doorway, later, from the porch of the great House.

"Mama, why all the hills?" five-year-old Lucy would ask. Mama would say, "Cause the good Lord wanted them all."

Sometimes the answer satisfied, sometimes it did not.

"Mama, I want to go see what over those hills."

"No, Lucy chile, you gonna stay right here. This is where you belong."

"Why Mama?"

"'Cause the good Lord put you here." Mama had Lucy nearly convinced of it. Before she was five, the Quarters, cabins on the Redmond plantation, were the whole world to Lucy. This is where Mama hoed corn, picked off tobacco worms, put in the hemp.

1

Then one day, the world changed. Mama told Lucy that they would move up to the great House.

"Why Mama?"

Mama looked out over those hills. "Guess it be what the Lord wantin' now."

Lucy asked, "Is it what Massa wantin' too?"

Mama sighed, "Sometimes it seem they be the same. The Missus gone now and Sally too old. Massa needin' us up at the House to do the cookin'"

Lucy's world widened, no more just the perimeter of the cabin. She had been scared of the huge pristine House with its wide verandas and columns. Her bare feet missed the dirt. Mama was impatient now and fussed at Lucy and Narcissa often.

They slept in a loft above the summer kitchen that connected to the House. Lucy and Narcissa learned a lot that summer she was five and Narciss three. They learned to tiptoe and whisper. They learned that chores needed tended to right quick. And they learned, most importantly, that the white folks were awful peculiar people.

1860

"Lucy, what be keepin' you, girl?" Mama was hollering again. Lucy groaned. She had gone out to the smokehouse for a few minutes to fetch a ham and there was Mama needing her.

"I'm coming," Lucy grumbled, lugging the twenty-pound ham into the brick-floored kitchen. "I'm here."

Mama glared at Lucy. "What take you so long to fetch a ham?"

Lucy signed. "I saw a butterfly. It was blue with spots. You doan see those kind hardly ever 'round here."

Mama rolled her eyes. "We got fixin's to do for Massa's company and you out watchin' bugs? You fifteen, girl."

Lucy put the ham on the block table. She rubbed her wrist. "Sorry, Mama." Her mother softened and put her hand on Lucy's shoulder in a rare moment of compassion.

2

Lucy eyed the kitchen. "Where Narciss at?"

Mama set to work. "She be with Miz Susan. Now she thirteen, Massa give her to Miz Susan, be her own maid." Mama prepared the ham for baking and motioned to Lucy to cut potatoes.

Lucy frowned. Mama noticed. "You jealous or something?" Lucy scoffed, "No. Jus' Massa given' Narciss to Miz Susan. Don't like that. Miz Susan a snivelsnip. She'll boss Narciss' 'round and 'round like a top."

Mama shrugged, "Massa do what he want. Always did spoil his womenfolk."

"Well, I'd like to be spoiled jus' once," Lucy declared. Mama turned fierce. "You ain't nuthin' but a slave, girl. You askin' for trouble if you don't know your place. You a slave and you always gonna be one."

Lucy stood there, studying the knife in her hand. The sun's rays glinted off the blade in different hues. Her hand looked pearl-like gripping it. Why she was near as light as Miz Susan. Yet she stood here, doing kitchen work. Narcissa, nearly as light, stood waiting on Master's daughter, and both girls double-fold as pretty as the Master's spoiled brat. The unfairness struck Lucy to the heart, much as a knife blade would.

"It ain't fair!" Lucy cried.

Mama harrumphed, "Fair. What that got to do with anything?" She set her lips in a fine line. Lucy knew there was nothing on earth that could pry them open. Mama not talkin'; it was time to go see ol' Cissie.

It was Saturday evening. Massa's fancy company was finally satisfied, and Lucy was free for a few hours. She went to the Quarters where ol' Cissie lived in her ramshackle hut, which she claimed her mama built. Her mama had came from "Afrika" on a "great white bird" across the waters.

Ol' Cissie had strange ways about her. She was ancient enough to remember Massa Charles' daddy, and she had been on Redmond for so long she had seen everyone else born, except for old Jambrel. Cissie could not read, but she could count. She had told Lucy how old she was and taught Mama

3

the healing arts. She taught Lucy the things Mama didn't hold with, like knowing everyone's business on Redmond.

Lucy found ol' Cissie crouched over her fire, barefoot with some bracelet around her ankle. Lucy crouched too, to study it over a smoky fire. This time it had no locks of hair, just some flat stones brushed with soot symbols. Lucy coughed from the smoke and sat back.

"You want sumpin' from ol' Cissie?"

Lucy looked at the dark eyes regarding her. She wasn't exactly afraid of ol' Cissie, just wary. "Jus' come visitin'," Lucy answered. She studied Cissie's gray locks, woven in a braid and flattened across her head.

Cissie cackled, "You wantin' answers to those endless questions of yourn."

Lucy nodded. "You got all the answers, Cissie. Mama be like a stone unmovin'."

"She got her reasons. You be sorry some day, wantin' the answers. Some things better not knowin'."

Lucy's toe pushed at a pebble. "I miss the dirt. We got to wear these funny brogans up at the House."

"I's remember. I work up at the House in my younger days, 'til I get on in years. Be Massa Charles' nursemaid, I was." She said it proud-like. "What be in your mind, Lucy?"

"Well, Narcissa have to be a maid to Miz Susan now. I miss her. She's so quiet-like, Miz Susan trod all over her for sure. Massa jus' do what he want," Lucy grumbled.

Cissie's boney arms prodded her small fire with vicious jabs. "You come here to spout off or ask questions?"

Lucy watched the smoke ascend in wafts. "What you makin'? It smells."

Cissie nodded approvingly, as if Lucy had finally done right. "I's makin' a paste of 'possum for Annie's little fella. He got chiggers bad."

Lucy watched Cissie stir her thick gray paste on a flat metal sheet over the smoke. "Cissie, I jus' thought of this thing. Why my skin near like Miz Susan's and I'm not treated good as her?"

4

"'Cause you a slave and Miz Susan ain't."

"What's the difference?"

"'Cause Miz Susan had a white mama, you a black one that be a slave."

"Then why me and Narciss near as white as her?"

Cissie was quiet for a spell. When she opened her mouth, she made a sound. Lucy jumped. "You have light skin, but you ain't white. That be the way it is. Your mamas be different."

Lucy digested this. She watched Cissie spit on her paste and stir it with a stick.

"You wantin' to know more, you go ask your mama now. Ain't for me to tell." Cissie tended her concoction. She ignored Lucy. Lucy knew she was dismissed. She stood.

"Over there be a bucket of greens. Take 'em to the House when you go." Lucy grabbed the wooden bucket. Then she marched as on a mission.

Chapter 2
A True Shepherd

The mission was forgotten when Lucy reached the House. A horse stood riderless at the tying rack beside the curving stone-chip drive. Lucy wandered up to it. She stroked the brown neck. It reached its nose into her bucket for the greens. Lucy laughed.

"There now, girl. Get on along," hollered a voice from the porch. Lucy peered around the horse's head and saw a preacher man on the veranda. Massa Charles stepped out beside him. Lucy hurried on. *Some preacher man.*

Lucy found her mama banking the fire. "Lucy, you get that cold supper on in to the dining room. Massa's got company for the night. After that, you come on up to bed early tonight. Be ready for the preachin' tomorrow."

"Mama?" Lucy said. Her mama turned. Lucy noticed how tired she looked, how her smooth skin had aged. "You ain't goan down to the frolic, Mama? Heard they're meetin' and singin' tonight down in the Quarters."

"My, no, chile. Got no need for that. We only got need of the preachin'"

"Why, Mama?" Lucy was puzzled. *How could the stern white man give them what they needed? What did they need?*

Mama answered, "We need the Lord's words, Lucy. They be all we got. They gonna help us through this life. Only way we gonna make it here."

"Here?" Lucy echoed.

Mama looked sad. "Yes, chile. Here in this sorry life." Suddenly Mama roused herself. "Get on in there, Lucy. And give me that bucket. You always seem to be standin' 'round with a bucket in your hand!"

Later, in the dark recesses of the warm loft above the summer kitchen, Lucy lay awake. She listened to Mama's breathing. Circular thoughts chased themselves in her mind like dogs on a coon trail.

She could hear the voices down in the Quarters, joyful singing about getting on over to Jordan. Then tomorrow they would sing about the blood of the Lamb. Massa let his people have their frolics on Saturday evenings. He thought it calmed the blood, whatever that meant. Overseer Barnaby told old Jambrel that. On Sunday, everyone had to come hear the white preacher. They got better victuals and more rest. The white preacher told them Massa was a good man, a lot like Jesus. He would be their good shepherd here on earth, until they got to Heaven to the true Shepherd.

Lucy liked the picture that made. She trusted Massa. When she served him breakfast or cleared the table, she wished just once he would look at her and smile. But he never did. So Lucy dreamed about it. She wanted her shepherd on earth to like her.

But Lucy didn't care if the shepherd's daughter liked her or not. Miz Susan was spoon-fed. She tried to remember the Missus. She had been gone since Miz Susan was little. Lucy remembered the burial. It was the only time Lucy saw a man cry. Massa half-filled the grave himself, before he let family help. Even Jambrel and Overseer Barnaby got a turn. All out under the beautiful magnolia tree that looked like it wept.

Miz Susan didn't cry. She had been too small to know what all the goings-on were about. Lucy herself had only been five, as Cissie later told her. Shortly after, Lucy and Narcissa with Mama, came up to the great House to work. Lucy, also later, found out that Mama had once been house-help in her early days, and the Missus had sent her to the fields. Things always changin' Mama told her, same as the seasons.

Lucy thought about what she knew of her family. Mama was the youngest of seven children. Her folks died during the fever Redmond had years ago. So had two of Mama's sisters and one brother. The others had been sold off to pay Massa's debts. Mama had cousins, but she distanced herself from them when she became a house servant. "Better this way, " she told Lucy. When Lucy asked about her daddy, Mama became tight-lipped again. "It something you know when you older." *How old,* Lucy wondered? But Lucy did know Mama had been married to a man named John. He ran off and was whipped, then fell sick and died. He had not been Lucy's daddy and there had been no sorrow or regret in Mama's voice. It was a fitful sleep that finally claimed Lucy.

The white preacher was as white as the dogwoods blooming behind him and nearly as wide. He was dressed in black with a crumpled white shirt under a dusty frock coat. His face was pinched. Lucy wondered if his preachin' hurt his head the way it hurt her ears. She also wondered if he felt like some ministering angel with his booming voice meant to shake them to the core.

Mama listened intently, so Lucy fought off the spirit of dissention and dislike for the white preacher.

"Little children, you are treading upon the threshold of Heaven. The only way to find yourselves among those saved souls abiding there, is your service and loyalty to your beloved master. Serving your master in obedience is a virtue, one God recognizes and loves. For how can we expect God to take us in to His bosom if we have no part in humility and service unto those placed in authority above us here on this earth? 'For whatsoever a man soweth, that shall he reap.' Now let us sing a hymn."

Someone started "Are you washed..." and the rest followed suit. Lucy mumbled the words but her mind was troubled. It was the same preachin' she had heard all her life. Would Heaven be no different from earth? Would God be just another taskmaster? Surely not, Lucy sighed. She liked the good Shepherd image better.

That evening, Lucy sat before Jambrel with the others from the Quarters. Jambrel was learned, some claimed he could actually read, but Lucy wasn't sure. He knew the Scriptures like he breathed, and was what Lucy thought of as a hoary head. His wrinkles spoke of wisdom and his eyes had fire. Unlike Jasper, a slave whose eyes burned with a dangerous anger, Jambrel's fire was proud and magnificent. No matter his body was bent and crippled.

Lucy listened now as he told them about Daniel, who trusted God to deliver him from the lion's den.

"Don't you think he was scared? Shore 'nouf he was, he just a man. But the difference for him was he trusted God. He had faith God would deliver him. Faith that in God's own good time He's gonna deliver us. Then out of this lion's den we go, marchin' proud that God see fit to lead us out. We gotta keep the faith. In the right time, right way, God gonna deliver us!" He looked around warily, then added, "We all gonna git to that glory land. Amen now." While several "amens" resounded, Jambrel's eyes met Lucy's. He winked. Lucy smiled.

Chapter 3

1861

Moving

"Lucy, get these here corncakes in there!" Mama ordered. Lucy took the platter reluctantly.

"Massa in there hollerin' over border states and idiots in Washun'ton. I ain't wantin' to go in there yet."

Mama looked cross. "You don't get on in there, these here corncakes gonna be cold, then he'll have something worth hollerin' over!"

Lucy turned toward the dining room from the summer kitchen. Mama was almost more a force to be reckoned with than the massa. Lucy set the platter down before Miz Susan. She caught the tail end of the talk.

"… go ahead and marry. If we wait, I'll be an old maid! Please, Daddy!"

Massa looked up from his paper, distracted. "Susan, it's a fool time to get married right in the middle of a war. Man's got

11

to have a powerful good reason to ask for your hand in times like these."

"Wilson does, Daddy. He's going to have to do something. The substitute he had went and got himself killed! They'll be back, forcing Wilson to enlist. If we were married, it would set a lot better. If he had twenty-five slaves, he'd be exempt. Couldn't we do something for him? You know with both parents gone and his brother hogging the whole estate, he's destitute. He is my intended, Daddy." Charles Redmond looked across the room. Lucy thought he was focusing on the magnolia tree, where the missus lay buried. He often sat at the dining room table, gazing out that window at her grave. "Susan, a man ought to stand on his own two feet. I know you want to keep him out of harm's way, but maybe you're being selfish. Every other man around here has had to take a stand."

Miss Susan resorted to tears. "Oh, Daddy! I love him so much. If he goes to war, he's likely to get killed, I just know it!"

Lucy could understand her not wanting to let go of Wilson Hendricks, what with Miz Susan being a little on the plain side. If Mr. Hendricks didn't come back from the war, she might well die an old maid.

"Wilson has had an unfortunate set of circumstances inflicted on him, I agree. Have you thought how he'll support you, in the future?"

"Daddy! You have enough and more! I don't see why you can't help him, us, get started properly. You've got seventy-five negroes on this place."

"Susan, dowries went out of fashion quite awhile ago. What makes you think you're worth it?"

Susan broke into a smile. "Daddy, I know you're teasin'. Won't you just think on it?"

Master Charles studied the magnolia tree again. Lucy gathered the plates and hurried back to the kitchen. She went to Mama, who was bent over the kettle on the hearth.

"Mama, heard Massa's talk. Maybe he gonna let Miz Susan and that Hendricks fella marry and give 'em some slaves.

You think he be serious?"

Mama didn't answer. She tucked a strand of stray hair under her kerchief. Lines framed her upper forehead. "Don't know, chile. Hard tellin' anything Massa do."

*   *   *

Lucy and her mama, Angelina, and Narcissa were leaving the Redmond plantation. Massa Charles had given them to Miz Susan as a wedding present. Lucy could have cried, if she had been given to such luxuries.

Lucy and Narcissa went to see ol' Cissie before they left. "Oh, Cissie, I'll miss you so much." Lucy hugged the boney old woman tightly. Cissie held Lucy, then backed up to look into her eyes.

"You doan forget to be strong. You do what's right, what your heart tell you. The right thing ain't always easy, especially in these times. It gonna take a powerful lot of strongness."

She hugged Narcissa and told her, "You doan forget now you named after ol' Cissie. That way you take a little of me with you." Both girls marveled over Cissie's words. They were always learning something new. They accepted her gifts, little cloth bags full of some smelly mixture. "Ward off the sickness." Then they went to see Jambrel.

His aged head was bowed. "There always partin's in this here life. Times gonna git harder 'fore they git better. Be strong. Do what's right, you hear now? Jesus help you, girls. He be the only true Shepherd."

Chapter 4

1862

Clover Hill

Things were always changing. All except for the wooden bucket in Lucy's hand–that remained the same. It was 1862 and Lucy had lived seventeen springs. None of that mattered to Lucy. She only knew things had changed and not for the better.

Massa had indeed given Lucy and Narcissa and Mama to Miz Susan, now Missus Hendricks, who had married Wilson Hendricks and moved to a small farm called Clover Hill, east of her daddy. Massa Charles had bought the place and supplied the couple with Lucy and family, one manservant, Gilbert, and ten field hands.

They had a fancy kitchen with a big black stove now. There were new kettles and skillets to season. Mama cooked for the Hendricks and also the field hands, who slept down in a one-room cabin by the pasture. Lucy's work had increased as well. She was to take water to the field slaves, mid-morning and mid-afternoon, besides cooking and serving in the House. In between times she was to clean, since Missus Hendricks was low on servants.

The night they had come, several months ago, Mama had pulled Lucy down beside her on her pallet. "Listen, girl, none of your questions. Jus' listen and do what I say. You stay clear of Massa Hendricks. Doan look at him, no matter what. You keep your eyes down in front of the Missus too, show respect now. Things gonna be alright iffen you listen."

Lucy had nodded. It didn't seem no different than back home. Why was Mama so stern with her words? Lucy knew all these things.

She toted the heavy water bucket to the field edge, careful not to slosh any out. The hands came over eagerly. Mama had told her not to be too friendly out here either. The men were all older, near the age her daddy would be, if she had one. They were kind to her and her heart warmed to them. All except the youngest one, named Rudy. His teasing made Lucy uncomfortable, although she wasn't sure why.

Today there were low murmurings about the war, about the blue-coated army that was on the move. Lucy had heard the talk, how lots of slaves were up and following them. *What would an army do with slaves,* she wondered, *'cept make 'em work?* It puzzled her.

Lucy had avoided Rudy. She took her empty bucket back toward the house. She swung it around in a wide arc until the remaining drops fell on her face. It made her smile. She looked up to see Massa Hendricks standing by the fencerow. He was watching her. Lucy ducked her head and hurried inside.

Lucy sure missed ol' Cissie and Jambrel. She even missed Massa Charles. And Narciss. She hardly ever saw her sister. Missus Hendricks was with child now and constantly dissatisfied. Narcissa would rush into the kitchen, near tears, for some tea for Miz Susan. Mama would take a cool cloth and wipe Narciss' forehead and speak soothing words to her. Mama was always gentle with Narciss. Lucy did not resent it; there was something special between them. Lucy felt too sorry for her sister to mind. She knew how hard it was waitin' on the

16

white folks.

They were contentious. Often the Massa and Missus Hendricks had words. She overheard the missus tell Massa she would have "no dallying around", that she wouldn't put up with it like her mama had. For newlyweds, they were often sharp with each other. Massa Hendricks was moody and not nearly the gentleman Massa Charles was. He always lorded his authority over his slaves like he had something that needed proven. Lucy wondered if this was why Missus Hendricks was unhappy with him most times.

Lucy kept her eyes and ears open that summer and fall. There had been little noticeable effect from the war, there on the farm. Clover Hill was missing out. Lucy never got off the place, but she knew Massa Hendricks had applied for another substitute to fight in his stead since he failed the requirement to own twenty-five slaves. And he had yet to make allegiance with the Union.

Fortunately, they grew their own food and had their own animals, but the staples were inflated. Massa fussed over flour, sugar and salt. Even coffee was harder to come by at two dollars a pound. Mama had taken to making her own with chicory. The Missus' tea was at ten dollars a pound as well, so Mama used dried berries and wild mint.

Lucy's world stretched with the names of places she over-heard Massa talk about at the table. Places like Bull Run, Fort Donelson, Malvern Hill, and Antietam.

In the spring of 1863, more interesting news made it to Clover Hill. Massa pounded the table with a massive fist over a place called Camp Nelson. It was a Union supply depot being built right over in Jessamine County beside Hickman's Bridge.

"Too blamed close," Massa Hendricks grumbled. Some general, Ambrose Burnside, had ordered the depot built as a central hub for his troops pushing south. Lucy recognized early on Massa Hendricks wasn't too fond of the Union army and its proximity. He voiced his fear to the missus that the blue-coats would steal slaves away for labor.

The field slaves were full of excited talk. Lucy heard of

something she could hardly pronounce, the Emancipation Proclamation. It said the slaves would be freed by President Lincoln at the beginning of the year. The question to them all was how and when? Lucy heard Massa say smugly that Kentucky, being a border state, didn't have to answer to that paper, that Lincoln had to coddle Kentucky.

Rudy, the mouthiest, said "Linkun is gonna have to cum down heah and free them all hisself" since Massa Hendricks was such a "pigheaded rebel". Rudy claimed they were taking slaves, "impressin' 'em" and using their labor on the roads for the camp. "Slaves jus' up an' runnin' away to help, smart ones that is."

Lucy worried over such talk. She would look around to see if Massa was near. Anymore, he always seemed to be lurking about. He gave Lucy smiles, but not the ones she had coveted from Massa Charles. Maybe he thought Lucy would tell him what the slaves said; be his spy. Maybe that's why he was hanging around and watching her. Well, she wouldn't tell him nothin'. She knew his blue eyes were both crafty and brazen. Mama would say he was a fox huntin' a henhouse.

On Sunday, the preacher, whose sympathies lay with the Kentucky slave-holders, told Wilson Hendricks some more news. Lucy heard it as she carried platters of greased greens and fried potatoes into the dining room.

"They're impressing slaves right off their farms to build the roads running into Camp Nelson over in Jessamine County. Talk of taking the railroad from Nicholasville on out too."

Massa Hendricks forked potatoes into his grim mouth in hasty motions. Lucy knew he was irritated. She hurried with the coffee.

"The report was three hundred dollars in compensation for each slave used, but I'd believe it when I see it. We hear General Morgan may be through here soon. He'll send these Yankees packing, maybe hinder that camp business too. He's put the scare around here more than once."

Lucy wondered over the preacher's talk. It didn't sound like his sermons any. He worked his collar away from his

Adam's apple.

"Worse is the slaves just taking off, just up and leaving their homes. Just shows how little mentality they got."

Lucy cleared the plates and brought in dried apple pie. She refilled the coffee cups.

Massa Hendricks finally spoke, "Reckon they'll bring 'em back after they see they'll need to horsewhip 'em to get any work done. Three hundred dollars talks. My pockets could use a little lining. I say let 'em try. Jinx on the Yankees." Both men laughed at his joke.

Lucy stood with herself flat to the wall and tried to look as uninterested as possible.

"Best part of this whole fiasco is Kentucky's position as a border state. She's too important for Lincoln to mess with. Any farmer who claims allegiance is exempt from those fanatical policies in Washington. Our property is secure since Lincoln's hands are basically tied."

Massa leaned forward. "But I'm not claiming no allegiance to that back-handed Union." He eyed the preacher hard.

" 'Course not, Wilson. Just a little knowledge and maybe a thought. In these times, we need to keep an open mind at our disposal."

Master Hendricks leaned back in his chair. "Good sermon this morning, preacher."

"Why thank you, sir. How is your lovely wife?"

"She's in confinement now. Clover Hill is about to expand." As both men made conversation on a new level, Lucy cleared dishes and carried them to the kitchen. She gave Mama a look. Her mother came close, bringing hot water.

"More news. Not sure what it's meanin'." Mama nodded and cut soap flakes into Lucy's dishpan. Mama seemed to brush off news, but she listened. That's how Mama was.

"Here," Mama instructed, shoving a wooden bucket at Lucy. "Go fetch more water. Those two men made more dishes than royalty."

Chapter 5
The Lashing

Lucy set her bucket down and clucked to the hens, who were on their way to becoming very precious. There were only a dozen left. Massa had wanted fried chicken, so Mama had wrung two of their necks. Lucy searched the nests for eggs when she heard the henhouse door close. She looked over her shoulder and saw Massa Hendricks standing there. She turned. "Oh, Massa, it you. You needin' something?"

He saw her hands full of eggs and motioned her to empty her hands into the bucket. Lucy hurried and put her eggs in it and stood. Thinking it was Miz Susan's time, she asked, "It be Missus Hendricks?"

"No," he said smoothly, "it's not Mrs. Hendricks." He moved towards her. Lucy was startled. His blue eyes had a strange light in them. She was suddenly afraid. "Massa?"

He grabbed her wrist and swung her around until she smacked the wall, sending dust and feathers into the stifling air. He gave a throaty laugh. Lucy's mind fumbled for some escape. She heard herself praying, but the words did not reach her lips first. Massa did.

Suddenly there were footfalls outside the henhouse. Narcissa's voice called out frantically, "Massa, Massa! It be Miz Susan's time!" Momentarily her feet echoed on. Massa Hendricks swore. He shoved Lucy toward the egg bucket and sent it flying against the wall. The hens, unsettled, squawked and flew up. Feathers met the air. Massa shouldered the door open and was gone. Lucy heard his black gelding tearing out the yard for the doctor. Her legs shook. She retrieved the bucket. It was splattered with egg. One wood-shingled side was loose, straying away from the metal band that secured it. Lucy took the bucket to the well. She washed out the egg mess and carried the broken bucket to the pasture. Beside the fire ring in front of the field hands' cabin, she set it down. They would know what to do with it.

She went into the kitchen and lowered herself into a chair for the first time all day. It was quiet. Mama was not about. Then Lucy remembered. Miz Susan's baby was on its way.

Mama came bustling into the kitchen. "We need hot water on to boil, girl. Why you sittin' there?" She looked at Lucy peculiar-like.

Lucy stared at the floor. She didn't move. Mama looked closer at her daughter. Lucy's pale face alarmed Mama as she knelt before her. She felt her trembling.

"Lucy, chile, what be wrong?"

Lucy's distressed eyes gazed into Mama's. She wailed, "The eggs all broken, Mama. Bucket is too. All broken." And with that, Lucy herself broke down and wept.

*   *   *

Lucy stiffened when Massa Hendricks came into the kitchen. She was now afraid of the man she served. Mama wasn't. Her words were sharp. "What you needin'?"

Massa motioned at Lucy. "You come out here and take your punishment for breaking my property. There ain't no excuse for waste in wartime." He grabbed Lucy and pulled her out to the yard. The field hands were assembled there, along with Gilbert, his servant. Suddenly Lucy understood! The broken eggs and bucket!

"I'm going to make you an example of a slave who breaks things and shows disrespect towards their master." He spit this out venomously and loudly for all to hear. Lucy cowered. Several field hands coughed and some shuffled nervously. Mama's hands were clenched and her face paled.

Quietly, Miz Susan had stepped out on the porch. Narciss stood behind her, the baby nestled in her arms, her eyes wide. It grew still.

"Mr. Hendricks!" Miz Susan called out. He slowly turned toward the porch at her voice.

"My daddy never had no need to whip his slaves publicly. If you must do this thing, you will take her to the barn. There's no cause to be indecent." Her eyes were hard and unwavering.

Massa Hendricks stood studying the sky, his lower lip clenched between his teeth. Finally, he nodded and prodded Lucy towards the barn. "Y'all get back to work. Now!"

In the barn, he advanced on Lucy where she stood stock-still. Terror of the unknown gripped her. With one strong hand, he gripped Lucy's kerchiefed head and turned her until she faced away from him. His voice was low, near her ear. She felt his breath. "You gonna learn I'm your master. You do my bidding." Then Lucy fully understood. This was not about civil property but about his fleshly property. He would force her submission. *Good Shepherd, where are you,* she pleaded.

She felt his hand on the back of her neck. With one sharp jerk, her dress back gave way. The fabric was old and worn and offered no resistance. Lucy gasped. Then she steeled herself.

The very first lash she heard before it struck. The pain of it made her mind go blank; white hot lights flashed across her eyes. The next strike she screamed. By the third, she fell to her knees—the air gone from her lungs. Still he didn't stop. She crawled for the hay, toward the patient-eyed cows that were alert to her distress. They were wary, their cuds still.

Hendricks raised the whip again, missing her back and striking her hip and skirts. Lucy screamed, "Mama!" but it

23

sounded like only a croak to her ears.

But suddenly, Mama was there. Unbeknownst to Lucy, her mama had not abandoned her. She had followed, torn by the desire to stop the madness from ensuing and to spare her daughter, yet unsure if she would be able.

"Massa," her voice rang from across the barn. "Massa, I'll make sure she don't break nothin' else." Her words were strong and commanding, penetrating Hendricks' angry upraised arm. He paused then and looked at Mama. He curled the whip up and tossed it along the wall.

"See she don't," he said curtly. He gave Lucy one glance before stalking out. Then Lucy felt Mama's wet face beside hers. Their tears mingled. Mama was crooning to Lucy, like she did Narcissa. "It's gonna be alright, baby, everything gonna be alright."

Now, Lucy lay on her side, sleeping, in their small room off of the kitchen. Mama had done up her back, putting poultices on it she had learned from ol' Cissie. She went to the one opened window they had, her dark hands clutching the frame. Gazing out, her eyes sought Jessamine County, where hope began to lay. Plans took form in her mind. Then Mama spoke quietly to Lucy's even breathing. "Jordan may be closer than we think, Lucy-girl. It's gonna be alright." Her eyes followed her daughter's still form. Slave mamas weren't foolish enough to promise their babies nothin', but Mama knew there was no choice left. They would reach "Jordan" one way or another, by foot or by wing.

Chapter 6

August 1863

The Escape

Wilson Hendricks had risen with the sun. He had no overseer, being what he considered a "poor" farmer. He stepped outside to the porch and breathed in the early morning air. His eyes followed the pasture, to the field beyond. The farm looked peaceful, not at all like the war-filled world around it. The encroachment from it was testing his patience.

Yesterday the army had requisitioned two of his best horses, but generously left him with one horse and the mules. The two pigs were missing and the cow had broken her leg. If this weren't enough, four of his slaves had been impressed two weeks earlier to build roads to the new camp. Then that young slave, Rudy, had taken it in his head to follow after and had run off. He had tracked him to the camp and fetched him back. After a good whipping, which had rendered Rudy useless for several days, Hendricks now had six workers, hardly enough to make a go of this rock-scrabble farm. It almost made a man bitter. The remaining field hands would just have to do the work of those missing. And

Susan would have to be content with her house help, such as it was. He regretted whipping that girl, Lucy. She hadn't amounted to much since and Susan was as fussy as their baby.

This war was beginning to squeeze him like one of those boa snakes. But he wouldn't give in. He would let the Union assume he was loyal and keep his slaves. Personally he believed states could do what they wanted; it was their constitutional right as far as he could see. Yet now the war, which began on this basic principle, was suddenly a war over slavery. He wasn't alone in his feelings, most of Madison County felt like he did. Now he heard they wanted to enlist blacks as soldiers. The Union was full of fool ideas. He noted he sure hadn't voted for Abraham Lincoln.

Wilson Hendricks came out of his reverie and strode to wake the field hands. On his way back to the house, he paused in the side yard. There was no smell of breakfast in the air, like most mornings. He watched for that pretty girl, Lucy, but she didn't appear. He went to the kitchen by the back door and looked in. All was quiet. He went in to the loft and called, "Angelina. Get breakfast on!"

There was no scurrying, no activity, and no sign of life. He tromped up the ladder until his head cleared the top. "Get up!" he called to the two humped figures, wrapped in tattered blankets. But they didn't move.

In two steps he was in the loft, jerking the covers back to reveal two rolled up blankets in place of bodies. It began to register things were amiss and another trouble loomed ahead of him. Like booming artillery, he stomped down the steps, thundering through the house calling for Gilbert, his manservant. Wilson questioned him on the disappearance of the kitchen-help. "No, Massa, I ain't seen nor heard anything. Don't know nothing about them being gone."

After this inquisition, he woke Susan. "Where's your girl? You seen her yet this morning?"

Sleepy, his wife struggled to sit up. She shoved back the frilly soft covers and went to Narciss' room off the hall. The baby slept peacefully. She came back into the bedroom, dazed.

26

"I don't understand. Where could she have gone?"

But Wilson Hendricks understood. "I think I know where they're headed." Camp Nelson was like a magnet. "They're just three women. I shouldn't have a problem overtaking them. Don't worry, Susan."

Susan Hendricks *was* worrying. Who was going to care for the baby, what would she eat, and how could she dress properly?

Her husband was pulling his shotgun down from the wall and stuffing ammunition in a cloth bag. "I'll go round up some of the neighbors to help. Ferguson has good dogs, we'll have them tracked in no time."

With a hasty kiss, he tore off, leaving brief instructions with his field slaves. He threatened them good, but the thought still nagged him they might take this opportunity to run off as well. He quickly dismissed it; with him out roaming around, there was no way they could slip past him.

*   *   *

When they finally stopped moving, Lucy's body did not obey her. She tried to bend, then sit, but in her weary state, her limbs were unyielding. She turned to Mama.

"Mama," she croaked. Mama took her arm and pushed her down beside a clump of ferns, onto a moss-covered boulder. Lucy groaned. Narciss collapsed at the base of out-cropping rocks, which loomed above them. No one spoke for a moment.

Mama seemed out of breath. "By Rudy's directions, we should be headed the right way." They had forded two streams and passed a bank barn.

Lucy nodded; it was all she could muster. Her head felt the weight of stone. Narciss seemed as dispirited. The night before, they had run. All night long and all this day, they had stumbled over briars and bushes and roots. The swarms of mosquitoes kept them company, feasting on their skin.

How far had they come? Lucy wondered but she had no way of knowing. The territory consisted of rolling hills, dressed with trees, which covered them well. Lucy was sure they must be getting close to Jessamine County and Camp Nelson.

Last evening came back like a haunting reflection. Unable to see clearly, it had been a terror for the three women. Owls hooted and the night creatures rose up, fluttery and swift, startling Lucy. The women would pause and listen for hounds. Yet this sound had been absent so far.

A sense of urgency kept them going, fueled by fear. Lucy ate, with no desire. Her innards recoiled at the dry crumbly biscuits and hard-boiled eggs. The cold salt pork even more so. Her hands trembled, nearly missing her mouth. But Mama made them eat for strength.

The fear of the unknown rivaled the fear of the known. If Massa caught them–. Lucy would force the thought from her mind. Mama had told them to succeed; they must focus on making it to the Kentucky River. It would take courage, raw unequalled courage, but they had little choice. Lucy knew she had to get away from Massa Hendricks.

Lucy's fear, like a cankerworm, ate at her until she felt physically sick. One look at Narciss confirmed she shared Lucy's turmoil. Yet Mama remained a pillar of strength.

They stopped that evening, at the outcropping of rock, and Mama studied it for some shelter. Her throaty voice was barely a whisper. "We'll sleep here tonight. Massa Hendricks probably tracked us all day, yet we're still safe. We haven't heard no signs of him. Let's crawl up on that shelf there and sleep until morning. If we're following right, we'll reach the river sometime tomorrow. Now you girls get on up there, and I'm going to broom away these tracks and hopefully the scent."

The girls obeyed. Mama took fern fronds and brushed around the area. Lucy would normally have noticed the Jack-in-the-pulpit flowers and the vines that wrapped themselves around solitary trees like snakes. Strange mushrooms grew in the rock's ledges and green velvety moss lined the shelf. Lucy and Narciss sunk on it, tense and unable to unwind. Small groups of midges swarmed them. The air felt heavy, like a wet fleece about their shoulders.

When Mama joined them, she gave them a care-worn

smile. "We don't see it, girls, but there be a pillar of fire over us this night. And all day long we were hidden under a cloud, protected by the Lord. You remember the story of Moses, don't you? We be just like the Hebrew children, leaving Egypt. And we're going to make it to the Promised Land." Mama said all this in a whisper and it made Lucy sleepy. She curled up, her apron a covered place for her head.

Mama's soft voice crooned on,

"We're coming, O'Lord, we're coming,
Send ol' Pharaoh away,
Cross over that sea,
We're crossin' over,
We're coming, O'Lord, to that promised land."

"We're doing this, girls, and we ain't never going to be sorry. We don't have nothing to lose, just everything to gain, girls. You trust Mama."

Lucy unraveled much like a skein of yarn and fell soundly asleep. She was dreaming she was in a pasture picking wild-flowers. Each one was precious, like a jewel. Each one had a different color. Mama had told her she must gather a bouquet of them, and then she could quit.

"Who's it for, Mama? Who we going to give it to?"

Mama would answer, but her voice was swallowed up in birdsong. Lucy could not read her lips and understand. So she would ask again, all the while picking her beautiful gems. Her arms grew tired, but she knew she must trust Mama.

Suddenly she was shook awake. She shrugged in her sleep, willing away the interruption. Mama's voice was low and urgent in her ear, "Lucy, there's dogs. I hear them. Wake up."

Lucy sat up, disoriented, but quickly able to grasp the seriousness of the situation. Even in the dark, unable to see Mama or Narciss, Lucy could feel their fear alive like electricity in the muggy air.

The hound's bays were distant, but they would find them, Lucy thought. They had crossed two small streams, not nearly wide enough to lose their scent. They had walked upstream a ways, but because it was so open, had sought the shelter of the trees.

Mama was praying, and Lucy supposed Narciss was too. Lucy knew it was the only thing left. They were sure to be found, and they had no recourse but to wait until it happened. To run more in the dark would be pure folly.

"God, you have to save us. Please keep those dogs away." Lucy paused. Mama told her you can't order God around. Lucy began bargaining with God. "Lord, save us and I'll live a godly life, always." Still Lucy's mind felt desperate and her heart more wrenched. "Shepherd, hear your lost sheep. Please keep those dogs from evil, your creatures from such sin. Spare us, Lord, if it be thy will." She thought of the Israelites in the wilderness. "Be our fire by night, God. Guide us to safety, please."

The three women prayed for minutes that became two quarters of an hour. The hounds grew nearer. Still Mama did not cease, and Lucy knew she believed in miracles. Lucy, too, would believe in them before the night ended. Her body was a well of sweat, yet her palms were ice-cold. She trembled uncontrollably, so that her arms seemed to grow numb. What waited ahead of them was such a mountain of evil that she could not face it. She simply put her face in her lap and repeated her petition to God.

The dog's barks and bays filled the woods, like knives slashing through the trees. Then closer they grew, until their voices were cut off. The dogs had grown silent. The three women forgot to breathe, so stiff with fright as they were.

Not far off, they heard men talking, high-pitched tones full of frustration. Lucy could not make out their words.

Then as if a volley had sounded, the dogs surged, their throats opened full throttle. Onward they tore, baying back to the east, on the trail of a coon. The riders had little choice but to follow, disgusted. Their horses' hooves became faint. Farther and farther away the sounds grew until the woods were quiet, save for the cry of a time-tricked song sparrow, announcing a too early dawn.

The three women collapsed upon themselves in a hug-held heap, and Lucy cried. *Had Moses ever felt this way?*

Chapter 7

A Miracle

When faint light crept through the trees, Lucy peered out. The trunks were dark, save the spaces between them where anemic shafts of yellow light filtered. Lucy breathed in the air–there was no menace in it, only kindness where God would dwell. Could the night have held such terror? A bird trilled and flew close to the rock cropping.

Mama crawled to the ledge and looked out. She spoke at last. "We'd best get moving. We got a river to follow today." She turned to Lucy. "We've had one miracle. I suppose the Lord can do another." Lucy nodded. She knew how Mama felt.

All day the undergrowth was bent on tripping them. Red-winged blackbirds called out in mocking tones. It seemed they moved from tree to tree, like shadows stealing, always as north-east as possible, following the sun. They stopped often to listen, but no foreign sounds entered the woods until early afternoon. At one such pause, they heard horses–clopping hooves jarred the ground and the jingle of harnesses met their ears. They crammed themselves down in the undergrowth. The bushy brush tugged at Lucy's skirts in spots and threatened to dislodge her head kerchief. But she lay as still as if dead.

The men were Union soldiers. They came near, almost to where Narciss lay hidden. A horse lowered its head and nickered, sensing their smell. The men were in cantankerous moods, paying little attention to their mounts.

"All I know is, I'm tired of patrol duty. If there's any of Morgan's Raiders around, I'd invite them to camp to spice things up a bit." The whiny voice was met by loud guffaws.

"You invite them! All they'd see of you is your waistband!" a deep voice jested.

"Come on, fellows. We got to get these horses watered. Rivers not too far now and it's nearly mess time."

Lucy listened and hope sprang in her heart, until one of the blue-coated men spoke. "You guys hear something?" The band of men grew quiet. Lucy dared not breathe. One of the men dismounted.

"I'm sure I heard something. Something that—." His voice trailed off as a reverberating noise descended from a nearby tree. Louder it became until a host of black and yellow roaring invaders penetrated the blue ranks of men. With an outcry, the men remounted and were cantering off. The swarm of bees seemed eager to pursue.

Now quiet reigned but the three women stayed hidden in the forest's undergrowth for a long time, hearts rumbling much like their deliverers.

When Mama felt safe, they crawled out and began their trek again, tree to tree. At intervals, Lucy would mentally offer up thanks. Soon the land slanted under their feet. It began a descent as though pulling them toward something. As the sun lowered, Lucy began to smell the air. It had a damp, fishy odor tinged with the smell of moist foliage. Then they heard it, a tumbling, rolling cadence that quickened them. Hurriedly now, they moved towards the sound, until the trees broke, and the sight they longed for had finally met their eyes.

Sparkling, silvery rivulets, laced with foamy skirts, rippled past rocks, merrily kissing gnarled tree roots. The misty slate colored water swirled by them. The center of the river held its surface calm, like a flat mirror. This was the river, the Kentucky River, that ran by Camp Nelson in all its magical glory. For moments, the three women forgot the chore of crossing it.

They sat, shoulder to shoulder, oblivious to their dangerous plight, simply gazing upon it. At last, Mama roused herself and pointed. "We have to follow it that way." Lucy looked at the sun. They must keep moving and figure out how and where to cross.

The sweat on Mama's brow reminded Lucy to wipe her own. Evening was here and they were close now, but could find nowhere to ford the river.

"Soon it'll be dark. We'll have to wait 'til morning to cross." The three women dreaded a night out again. Already Massa Hendricks had probably been close by and was maybe even lying in wait. They huddled on the bank of the river, near a gaping stump for protection. The water nearly wet their feet. Lucy pulled off her house brogans, in sore condition after their journey. Her feet were red and blistered. She soaked them along the water's edge and fell asleep. Narciss leaned against her, despite the heat.

The night was uneventful and Lucy woke to a crow cawing. The sun seemed high in the sky and startled her. Mama handed her their last bit of food, a stale piece of bread. Lucy swallowed it practically whole and remembered to thank God afterward. Mama frowned at her. Lucy looked at Narciss. She had not forgotten. Lucy sighed.

For several hours, they labored along the river, hugging the bank close for cover until Mama stopped dead in her tracks. Ahead on the river was a ferry. Blue-coated men enclosed it like fenceposts, as they operated the raft.

"Now what?" Lucy thought out loud. Mama sat down to collect her own thoughts quietly.

"Well, we don't got no money to cross, and I'm scared those men will ask questions. Maybe Massa Hendricks told them to watch for us."

Lucy wished they could swim the river but none of them knew how. She also wished they were men; then they could pose as workers.

"We need an angel," Narciss said.

"That and another miracle," Lucy added. She sidled up to Mama, who had hunkered down in the thicket. "What are you planning, Mama?"

Mama didn't answer. She was listening to something, turning her head. At first, Lucy thought Mama was praying, but she didn't shut her eyes. Lucy glanced at Narcissa. Sure enough, her sister's eyes were closed, but Lucy suspected she was only sleeping.

Mama opened her mouth but quickly snapped it shut. She pointed, pulling Lucy down further in the green foliage. Narciss woke and leaned close.

The sensation that met Lucy's person was an easy rumble, which shook the ground slightly. Next into view, came a wooden-sided spring wagon. Its massive wooden hubs and wheels rolling along like gentle stars out of orbit. Four mules pulled it; the impact of their hooves met the dirt road with a solid sound. Dirt swirled in eddies much like the river had. Over the broad-backed animals rode a teamster. The wagon was packed with crated boxes, barrels and carpetbags. And atop this conglomeration rode several people. Black people.

If Lucy had seen an actual angel, she could not have been more surprised. Before her eyes, one of the mules halted and lurched against the harness, then went down on its front legs. The driver pulled out a whip and began shouting at the creature. When this effort failed, he stayed his hand and clambered down over the wheel hub to the animal, grumbling.

Mama shook with excitement as the black people, two men and three women, also climbed down and stretched their legs. "I'm going over there, girls. See what this is about. You stay put." Before her daughters could protest, she was up the bank. They watched her skirt the driver, and approach the women.

The women's faces changed from surprise to pleasure at Mama's appearance. Lucy had never disobeyed Mama outright, but she had to get close to these people. She had to hear the words they spoke and know what this group meant.

34

She crawled up the bank, feeling Narciss clutching at her hem, only to let go and follow her. Cautiously she went, standing behind Mama, just close enough to hear.

"We're from Madison County on our way to Camp Nelson to join our husbands, me and Ruby. That's Ruby's girl. I'm Naomi. The men here are going to work on the railroad north of the camp. Where y'all from? Y'all runaways?"

Mama adjusted her head kerchief and tucked in stray hairs. She took her time in answering. "On the way to Camp Nelson too. Only need to ford yet. Is this a safe way, along with you folks?" Mama eyed the woman sharply, and then gestured to the busy teamster.

The woman was plump and jolly, but she raised her eyebrows seriously now. "Honey, you ain't got nothing to fear from our group. Our benefactor's an angel in the flesh. He's helped us this far, getting us loaded up along with his delivery here. You can cross with us. I'll talk to the teamster after he's done messin' with that critter there. He's got orders to take us to Camp Nelson and bein' paid good for it. Now tell me where you hail from."

Mama was cautious with her words, but she didn't want to offend their newfound friend. The other two women and men greeted her. The woman named Ruby said, "Let us help you with your things."

Mama met her eyes evenly. "I don't have things, only two daughters—". She saw all eyes behind her. She turned, seeing Lucy and Narciss. She narrowed her eyes at them and mumbled, "Guess we're all here now."

Lucy knew Mama was surprised they had disobeyed, but Mama was too happy to reprimand them.

One of the men was introducing himself to Narcissa. Mama quickly took over the introductions. Lucy hid her amusement. Her sister's discomfort was obvious, as was Mama's "mother hen" instinct.

Naomi went to talk to the white man, and Lucy stood close to Mama, disturbed. White men were so authoritative. Would the teamster agree to take them on and not ask questions?

What if Massa Hendricks would come along? Surely he would just turn them over. The more Lucy thought on it, the more frightened she grew. She messed with her dirty apron, balling it up and twisting it, until Narciss frowned at her.

Then suddenly they were climbing up the sides of the wagon. The taciturn teamster had surveyed the group and only shrugged. "Y'all on your own. You ride, I drive. I don't get paid to answer no questions, just do my job. Right now I aim to cross on that ferry." He boarded the wagon, and the load rolled forward.

Lucy had never ridden much on a wagon before, except from Redmond to Clover Hill. She clutched tightly the barrel she was on, unsure, but soon familiar with the motion.

While they traveled toward the ferry, Lucy was assailed with doubts. Suppose Massa was waiting at the camp? Maybe he had told the soldiers at the ferry to stop them. Lucy's thoughts were interrupted by Naomi.

"We up and left our Massa. When we got to Berea, he caught up with us, Ruby, her girl and me. We got to beggin' him to let us go after our men, but he was determined we would go back with him. He started hitting Ruby and tied my hands.

"Then along came this man and told him to set us free. Massa didn't take too kind to him, but he gave Massa money and gave us work papers and told him we was contracted. Massa then agreed. That man then marched us along and fed and housed us. He said he would be our benefactor and now we was contracted to the Lord. He told us, 'Go with my missionary parcels to Camp Nelson and you'll be free.' We just have to work for our keep there and we can join our husbands. He sent us on and here we are!"

She was finally out of breath. Lucy had listened with fascination but the wagon jolting to a halt drew her attention to the scene before her.

Two soldiers stood on either side of the mules and spoke to the teamster. He spit a wad of tobacco over the edge of the wagon.

"I'm getting paid to deliver these goods to the camp. I don't know anything about no runaways. These people came with my load to transfer. You ask them." He jerked a stained thumb towards the crowded company perched a top his cargo. They all sat silent.

One of the soldiers spoke, "We've got orders to only let men into camp. No women or children. There's been some men here looking for female runaways." He came closer to the side-boards. The teamster worked on another brown wad. He said nothing, looking ahead into the tree line with a bored expression. "Well? Are you transporting runaways?"

The teamster spit. "In broad daylight?" he snorted. "I get paid when I deliver, and I aim to do my job."

The soldiers ignored him. They came up to Lucy and her companions. "You runaways?" Lucy swallowed, clearly frightened. Everyone remained quiet.

"You all are going to have to get off. No women allowed in camp. Strict orders."

Now Naomi found her voice. "We've got work orders. Our benefactor sent us to come here."

"That so?" one of the soldiers, his face covered with sideburns and a full beard, sneered at her. "Guess your paper don't mean nothing, unless it's signed 'General Burbridge.' Your paper say that?"

Naomi stayed still. The teamster half turned in his seat. He looked hard at the group perched on his freight. "You women gonna have to get off. I got my job to do."

Lucy's rocketing heart plummeted to the pit of her stomach. She felt light-headed with fear. No one moved. Would the soldiers throw them off? Lucy soon saw they had no need. They simply raised their guns. There followed several clicks. When Lucy gazed into the soldier's eyes, the darkness there was more troubling than the black muzzles of the cocked guns. Lucy shuffled her skirts around to find footing.

"Hold there. What seems to be the trouble?" A forceful voice came from across the river, booming like a 12-pounder cannon. Lucy swung her face toward the sound, and fell on her backside upon a barrel. It rocked.

A white man stood beside a gray mare, his arm outstretched

with a riding crop. As if lightening had lit up the river in broad daylight, the man's angelic reflection fell across the water, stretched from bank to bank. The sun shone golden all around the ferry, casting a blonde hue on all their faces. The air felt charged with the supernatural. "Those people are my charges. Bring them over!"

Lucy's head swam. The man, like Moses, waved his riding crop for emphasis. His beard was not snow white and flowing, but gray sprinkled with silver streaks and cropped at his collar, but it had the same effect. He wore only his white shirtsleeves, his coat thrown over the mare's saddle, but to Lucy he appeared as if in a white robe. Lucy expected the Kentucky River's waters to part and reveal a dry bed of pebbles beneath.

The soldiers lowered their weapons and mumbled whispers to each other. They knew this man and clearly felt submissive to him. Lucy wondered what manner of man he was.

The men backed off and the teamster drove onto the raft. Lucy scrambled back to her original perch, her eyes glued to the white man on the opposite shore. As the ferry floated away from the banks and bobbed, Lucy tore her gaze from the man to the water. The river was dark now, like black glass. The ferry rocked and jetted around, the soldiers poling them toward the opposite shore.

When Lucy snapped her head up, the Moses-man was gone. There was no sign of him or his sway-backed gray horse.

She bit her lower lip, her mind processing the fact they were crossing the river and how tenuous this feat had nearly been.

When the raft bumped the bank, they were pulled tight by heavy ropes which two soldiers secured around poles the size of tree trunks. The teamster gave a whip-crack and the mules pulled into the harness. Creaking, the wagon started uphill, all intact. Lucy cast a backward glance over her shoulder to meet smoldering eyes. She promptly turned back around.

Naomi whispered excitedly, "That's him! That's our benefactor man."

Mama nodded. They were all too astonished to say anything. Their mysterious angel was gone.

Chapter 8

The Camp

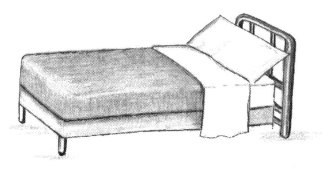

The rise up from the river rose to nearly vertical. Limestone rock embraced a little road of dust that, in staircase fashion, ascended to the top of the cliff.

The teamster's whip cracked harshly, along with his voice, urging and driving the teams toward the top. At one point, the wagon's occupants leaped off and walked alongside the animals to lighten their load. Lucy was glad to loosen her muscles, which had been severely clenched. When they mounted the rise, Lucy shared the sweat the animals exhibited, though their bodies were lathered in white foam from the exertion.

And then, there before them lay the camp, spread out like some flaming host, a sprawling labyrinth of intricate arrangement. Lucy clutched the wagon sideboards tightly, her awed eyes absorbing the scene. The vision, like a minute morsel of freedom, was tantalizing to the core of all their beings. Lucy swallowed hard.

Clusters of buildings lay fortified and girded in white, looking for all the world like the New Jerusalem to Lucy. Strong perimeters of wooden split-rail fence enclosed whitewashed and yellow pine board buildings. Honey-lemon shingles adorned the hundred structures. White symmetrical tents spilled across the swelling rises like shorebirds. Then, as a river's surging waters, blue-coated figures became a slightly perceptible movement, canvassing the parade grounds.

They drove to the camp's gates and were halted. A score of men loitered around but only two came up to the teamster. They looked over his load and at Lucy's group. They spoke to the teamster in low tones, and he gave them a receipt of some kind. The short, dark-haired soldier handed it back. Lucy held her breath.

"You can bring in the goods and the men, but not the women. General's orders."

Naomi, quick on the draw, was flourishing her papers. "We're contracted, same as the men. Work orders!" Her wrinkled papers fluttered like a bird with broken wings. The soldiers eyed them with distaste. One shrugged. "Heard Fee had some shipment coming."

"Looks like more of the usual." He rolled his eyes. "Let Quartermaster Hall deal with it." Lucy's toes were scrunched up in her tattered brogans in a show of will. They just had to be admitted.

The guards stepped aside, looking away, assuming no responsibility. The wagon rumbled forward. Mama and Narciss' faces were etched with relief. Lucy exhaled, nearly spent.

Across the grounds they rode. The soldiers paid them no mind. Frequently dark men at work would study the load with searching looks. The disappointment in their faces touched Lucy. Decidedly, she studied the buildings to avoid the sorrow.

In front of one such building, the teamster stopped, a clue for the group to dismount. He drove on, around the side of the structure, with no farewell or backward glance. There was obviously no sentiment in teamsters.

Bewildered, the group was suddenly rescued by a woman. Willowy was the description Lucy came to at first glance. The woman was definitely black, her pecan skin glowing just like the smile that wreathed her face. Her hair was pulled atop her head, fixed much like a white woman's. No head kerchief covered her. But her eyes were the most drawing, two orbs of bluegrass, regarding them kindly.

She pointed the men in the general direction they should go to contract work and turned her attention to the women. She regarded Naomi's papers with a smile.

Lucy's eyes never strayed from the calm, poised woman. Why, she hardly looked older than Lucy herself!

Lucy suddenly was aware of her filthy garments so evident before the woman's crisp, clean attire. Lucy wanted to cringe and tears pushed at her eyelids, unbidden.

While Naomi was giving the introductions, Lucy's eyes met those of the kind stranger. They held only friendship. Her pleasant voice spoke, "We'll let you all use the bathhouse, and I'll find changes of clothing for you that need it.

"I'm Miss Melinda Fair, with the American Missionary Association and I help out where I can here. I'm also a matron at the housing cottages, where the other women dwell. Their husbands are here working and they've come to join them. That's where I'll be taking you presently.

"I'll just talk as we walk along. Are you joining husbands here?"

Naomi and Ruby were nodding while Mama, silent, looked guarded. Miss Fair cast a sharp eye on Mama, but she didn't miss a heartbeat in speaking. "I'll explain our situation here, ladies. This camp has provided our people with opportunity. Some of the men running it are aware of that and overjoyed, some of the men are not. I think we can make our situations work for the best. I hope–." She hesitated. "The U.S. government has opened avenues for our people. They have made our men actual soldiers in some states. I hope we can expect that for Kentucky too."

She stopped and pressed close. "Listen. To anyone who's run away, there's room here for you. There is no shortage of work, especially women's work. Men will look the other way for a full belly and cleanly pressed clothes. What I'm saying is, lie low and work hard and I think you'll be fairly safe. We are some of the first women here. At times they try to round up the women and send them back where they came from. But still, there's a need for us here. Quartermaster Theron Hall is not unfeeling, and I think he'll help any of us out. Aha, here we are."

Lucy gazed at the square wooden building. After entering as if through a maze, she stared at several metal tubs of cool water. Miss Fair passed out cloths and soap. "Just scoot your clothing out under the walls." She motioned to the wallboards which rose a foot above the dust.

With no ceremony, Lucy began to comply. Modesty did not seem a privilege just now. Narciss was studying the water to see if it had been previously used. Lucy poked her. "You goose! Just get in!" Lucy shoved her clothing under the building.

Outside the bathhouse, gingerly looking at the stained, filthy garments and taking mental notes on sizes, Miss Fair gathered them all into a burlap bag, heartily dooming it to the burn pile.

Lucy took up her soap and turned when she heard gasps. Startled, she swiveled to see Naomi and Ruby, with her daughter, looking stricken. When Lucy realized that she, herself, was the cause of it, panic smote her. She remembered her scarred back and quickly hid it from their looks of pity, lest it undo her. She was suddenly ashamed. "Mama," she pleaded.

"It's alright, Lucy. We all know what it's about. We all have black skin and we all know. Now let's carry on here. We can't have Miss Fair waiting on us." It momentarily ended the awkwardness, but Lucy was bothered by the tears dripping off Naomi's chin. She struggled to maintain her privacy.

Soon the women were corralled by Miss Fair and led to Housing #8. Lucy kept running her hands over her clean skirt and shirtwaist. They felt so good. "Just things from the mission barrel," Miss Fair had said. In a brave moment, Lucy felt she had shed her old skin, ready for whatever was ahead of her.

"Come in and pick an empty cot, ladies. Get some rest. We'll tour the grounds tomorrow, and I'll secure work for you. We've a great progress happening here, and we're all going to be a part of it. You'll see."

Lucy stood at the foot of the cot. Made up beneath a coarse, gray wool, army blanket, lay snow-white sheets as glorious as anything Lucy had ever seen. She sighed as her fingers stroked their smooth coolness. She longed to slip under them as if they were a saint's white robe, and after a moment's hesitation, she did.

Lucy lay on her magnificent bed, and she knew she wanted to see Miss Fair's vision. But more than that, she wanted to see this camp as a safe haven, away from Massa Wilson Hendricks, safe as the white sheets seemed to promise. The sleep of exhaustion should have claimed her, but worried thoughts assailed her like little soldiers upon her army-issued wool-blanketed cot.

Would they be safe here or would Massa Hendricks come to take them back to Clover Hill? Would they be sent out of camp or would they be able to blend in and find work as Miss Fair said?

In a dream state, the Moses-man's face appeared to Lucy. She questioned who he was as sleep overtook her. Her lips moved but no sound escaped. In her unconsciousness, Lucy, herself, wielded a stout rod and parted the way before her people.

Sunlight woke Lucy. She sat up, disoriented, the room strangely filled with cots and see-through windows, shiny as the sun itself. Women moved around making the ten beds on each side of the room. In the middle of the cottage was a door, which led down a set of railed steps, as the cottage was built slightly above ground. At one end of the room sat a black rotund wood-stove, looking like a belching toad on squat legs. At the other end, a modest pine nightstand sported a white washbowl and pitcher. Two towels of linen lay beside it.

Miss Fair and Mama came into view. Mama smiled at Lucy as she sat down on the edge of Narcissa's cot to wake her. Ruby and her daughter went to the washbowl.

"Good morning, Lucy. You remember me?" Miss Fair smiled good-naturedly at Lucy's bewildered expression. Lucy rubbed a hand over her face and nodded.

"I'll let you wash and take you to breakfast. We'll eat at the mess hall, behind the kitchen. Then I'll take you all on a tour of the camp."

As Lucy straightened her cot and used the washbowl, she marveled at Miss Melinda Fair. What made a single woman, who appeared well bred, become a member of the American Missionary Association and work at Camp Nelson? She was undeniably attractive, her skin several shades darker than Lucy, and magnetic green eyes, the shade of a peridot. Lucy also envied her smile.

What an enigma Lucy's surroundings had suddenly become, and unfortunately, she had out-grown her inquisitive stage. Mama's disapproval had become a strong deterrent. She was simply too old for it anymore.

Lucy honed in on Miss Fair's voice. She was talking to Mama, "...question the ethics of men. But there are some men, behind the scenes, who restore your faith in mankind once more."

Lucy stood and returned Miss Fair's smile, letting its excitement buoy her as they left the cottage.

But Lucy's rash excitement faded quickly into a docile fright. She had never seen so many men and mules, never heard so much noise and ruckus, and never felt so many reverberations and rumblings. It seemed a lot like the description of the end of the world Lucy had heard preached. Only no, Miss Fair had joyfully asserted, this was all just a beginning. Lucy stood close to Narciss, bumped into Miss Fair often, and stood on Mama's feet. The tour was overwhelming and Lucy could keep nothing straight. Her senses felt assaulted. Melinda pointed, "Over there is the White House, the officers quarters, and to the left, Quartermaster Hall's office. On the right, the soldiers' barracks, the prison, then the parade ground. The blacksmith, mules, corrals, and stables all reside in that direction. You probably all came by the hospitals."

44

When the tour ended, Miss Fair let them rest and went to secure work for them. "A place for everyone," she had smiled. Lucy knew Miss Fair could move mountains with that beam of hers. But Lucy felt she had no beam of her own. In this new environment, she felt more uncertain than ever. She sank on her cot and closed her eyes and dreamed of Redmond.

Chapter 9

September 1863

A New Life

Lucy soon had no reason to dream of Redmond. Like spokes that propel a wheel forward, the camp rolled Lucy steadily toward a new life.

Lucy, Mama and Narciss became washerwomen for several days a week. They also worked in the mess hall for the head cook, Sammy, doing kitchen chores, as well as in the bakery. Lucy scrubbed dishes with a vengeance, uniforms with vigor, and potatoes with a purpose. Her life's work suddenly had new meaning, one with a sense of freedom, far different than enslaved work had been.

And like a rolling wheel, Camp Nelson was rightly christened a "hub" for the Union armies. Lucy came to learn that it was a supply depot, training center, and gathering place for the fortunate Federal army by orders of General Ambrose Burnside. Miss Fair had shared with Lucy that the camp's namesake, the notable General William Nelson, had certainly made the news when he defeated Kirby Smith at the Battle of Richmond. His recruiting skills had been noticed by President Abraham Lincoln. He had established Camp Dick Robinson, earning him recognition among his peers. But after death, he had reason to smile with this significant "hub" named in his honor.

The Camp had 300 structures in the form of hospitals, nurses' quarters, forage sheds, corrals, stables, mess halls, soldiers' barracks, quartermaster warehouses, commissaries, and refugee buildings, and, in the winter of 1863-64, a Soldier's Home. There were wagons and ambulances, horses and mules, (both serviceable and unserviceable).

Lucy came to witness that the many tools, forage and fodder, ropes, straps, buckets (many of which she came to carry), and harnesses and bridles were often manufactured right in the camp.

The camp's water was reported of good quality, first being hauled in wagons from the Kentucky River, but soon relegated to a supply tank and pump well situated along the cliff at the river.

Camp Nelson was a hub for deeper, more intricate reasons, not all realized in Ambrose Burnside's time or even quite clear to Lucy. She had heard read the words written aforetime: "Love thy neighbor as thyself," and "whatsoever ye would that men should do to you, do ye even so to them". These thoughts did not revolutionize freethinking, but spoke to the heart of man, universal and eternal. Lucy had been taught to abide by them. Suddenly here in camp, there were others who did too.

Humanitarian efforts born at Camp Nelson to better Lucy's people through aid, schooling, and preparation for the future in a post-war country were by no means an easy feat. Despite lurking opposition, progress was made because the actual silent hub was God's love–a simple concept recognized if the heart was right.

Lucy found many right hearts. There would be one behind the hearts who gave them their steady beat, which Lucy was soon to discover, one who Lucy had not imagined.

But tangible to Lucy were the people who manifested such principles daily, like Miss Fair and Quartermaster Hall. Others who made up Lucy's new world were Sergeant Ribford, the work crew manager, who was jolly and easy to work for; and Lucretia, a mother of three little ones in cottage #8, who was always pleasant, even when her baby had colic or when she only saw her man an hour each evening. Cook Sammy was always blustering about some over-cooked mess but while the words came out one side of his mouth, the other side hid a smile. And then there were Naomi and Ruby.

Within this tight circle, Lucy's fear of Massa Hendricks coming to retrieve them began to fade. She did not mind the wash detail or cooking in the mess hall. The work had new meaning. Miss Fair was true to her word. They were some of the first women in the camp, and they were needed. "Just wait and see," Miss Fair had urged, "Camp Nelson is going to keep growing. There's work for everyone!"

When Lucy had first come to camp and seen the fresh-sawn lumber going up and smelled the woodsy sawdust in piles, little would she realize how symbolic it all was. Her own life was comparable to this camp, new and constantly growing. How quickly the buildings went up! How quickly Lucy flourished because of her kind laboring compatriots!

Often amid the day's toil or night's reflections, Lucy would think of Naomi's benefactor, her own Moses-man. Who was he in this tenement of play? Where was he? When would she see him again, if ever?

Lucy learned not to fear the white soldiers. The black workers also minded themselves. This was, after all, an army post, most orderly. She went about her work, envisioning them all as a toiling colony of ants. All toward a good end, Lucy was sure. As time elapsed, winter came upon the camp, and Lucy and her family were warm, well fed, and Lucy chose to believe, relatively safe at Camp Nelson.

Chapter 10

Summer 1864

The Moses-Man

On the day Lucy heard the sermon, a big part of her became complete. It was like scraps of dough that, blended together pleasingly, make enough to roll out for another pie. Or, like bread dough rising, all the concave dents going convex, revealing a lovely leavened loaf.

This is how Lucy felt after hearing that sermon. In time it would change her existence, but on that early summer day, Lucy, in the army fashion of a double-quick two-step, began to embrace life.

The morning was perfect Kentucky weather, kind to its recipients. Lucy breathed in the roaming air with a tinge of river smell and sighed. She was on the steps of the cottage, in a hurry to get down to the schoolhouse for services. Seating was limited and lots of times they had to stand.

"Narciss, what are you doin'? Hurry on out here!" Lucy was

cross with her sister. Lately she had taken to spending a lot of time primping, all without a mirror, but primping nonetheless.

Lucy hollered again through the doorway, "What are you messing around for? You going courting or to church?"

Narciss appeared. Her hair was braided and wrapped around her head.

"Who you trying to impress?" Lucy was suspicious. "You look like ol' Cissie."

"Thanks! And you should take a hint, Sis. We're going to church. Wouldn't hurt you none to fix up a little. Your head kerchief clean?"

"Of course!" Lucy was ruffled. "You're trying to be late on purpose. You want people lookin' at us!"

Narciss didn't answer. Lucy continued, "Being late is for fancy white folks and you know it."

Narciss calmly insisted, "It don't hurt none to look nice going to church. Mama raised us proper."

Lucy's grumbles died. Narciss wasn't herself, that was for sure. She shook her head in disgust.

Once they arrived, they found Mama and all settled on a backless bench to Lucy's relief. It was much easier to listen if she were comfortable. She wasn't like Mama.

There was a different preacher man this time, Lucy noticed. He was white, of course, but something drew Lucy to look closer. He was speaking to Quartermaster Hall up front of the congregation. Lucy caught sight of his profile and her swallow stuck in her windpipe.

"Mama." She tightened her grip on her mother's arm. Mama grew inwardly silent, same as Lucy did.

The man, in gray suit cloth, was the Moses-man. Lucy trembled on her bench. Like an hourglass with its sands run out, Lucy felt a strange expectancy.

The Moses-man smiled at the crowd. His eyes glittered, not like knives, but like sparkly sunshine on raindrops. Lucy watched as he was introduced as the Reverend John G. Fee.

And then he spoke, his gaze lingering on the crowd by way of each individual, it seemed. Lucy found it wasn't hard to follow Reverend Fee. He believed the words he spoke and read in his black Book. Lucy saw it in his eyes and heard it in the timbre of his voice. There radiated such a love and compassion, Lucy felt it in the air between them, thick and soft, like sheep's wool. This man the sheep knew. This man was their earthly shepherd. The Moses-man image was suddenly replaced.

"You have heard before, dear ones, 'obey your masters' for this is your God-given duty, but have you heard 'Masters, give unto your servants that which is just and equal?' I trow not! Have you heard that God is a God of impartial love? That God sees into the hearts of men, no color barring, and cares for every soul born upon this earth? Have you heard God is no respecter of persons? That Christ is all and in all? That you, dear fellow servants in Christ, you are created in the image of Him who created us all? 'There is neither Jew nor Greek, there is neither bond nor free, male or female: for ye are all one in Christ Jesus.' These holy words of God are in this Book, which I hope soon all shall freely read for themselves.

"The distinction between us, here on earth, may be skin color, hair color, eye color, but God looks not on the outward appearance of man, but on the heart.

"What fills your heart today, loved ones? Is it hurt or fear, love or hatred? God is here for you today. 'He gave His only begotten Son, that whosoever believeth in him should not perish but have everlasting life.' Through Jesus' atoning blood we have hope.

"We all have a choice today, brethren. Where I grew up, I could have easily followed in my daddy's footsteps. I could have held myself over my brethren and committed sin. I could have refused to follow Moses' example, who left Pharaoh's house, 'choosing to suffer affliction with the people of God, than to enjoy the pleasures of sin for a season.' Come out from among the evils in the world, dear ones, choose to love rather than hate, free yourself from the bondage of hate by forgiveness, and let yourself be sanctified by Christ's blood. Each soul is precious to our heavenly Father, and we all deserve to accept this choice freely, unhindered by the bondage of fellow men.

Let us pray."

Lucy gulped and slid to her knees. What a fire burned, a light upon a candle, a flame stoked by an unseen Hand!

After services, the Rev. Fee met and encouraged the congregation, white and black alike. He talked with them all afternoon until his next sermon at evening. He saw hearts made clean, repentance sought, and acceptance that all men are created equal in the minds of the oppressed. He appeared tireless. Lucy had waited her turn in line, but when faced by Rev. Fee, she could only manage a shy greeting. The preacher's eyes said no matter. It was really the grasp of his hand Lucy had sought, to see if he was, indeed, real.

Lucy walked with Mama toward cottage #8 that evening after the meetings. Narciss had stayed to serve refreshments, but not without Lucy's raised brows aimed in her direction.

"Mama, how did you feel when Rev. Fee preached?" Lucy asked.

Mama gave her a sideways glance. "Why you askin' that?"

Lucy shrugged, "He's got something powerful about him."

Mama nodded, "He's armed with the Lord's spirit. Ain't nothing stronger."

"You always have believed them words, haven't you, Mama?"

"'Course. When you ain't got nothing else in this life, you got to believe."

Lucy pondered this. "You think we're as good as Massa? God loves us as much?"

"That's what the reverend said, didn't he? If you can't believe the simple things, you ain't going to believe the hard ones either."

"What's the hard ones, Mama?"

Mama was silent for a moment. "The hard ones is loving your neighbor and doin' good to those who 'despitefully use' you. Those are the hard ones."

Lucy persisted, "So if we are as good as Massa, why things the way they are?"

But Mama didn't answer. She had stopped, a salt pillar in her tracks, a replica of Lot's wife. "Lucy! Come quick, girl!" Mama grasped Lucy's arm and pulled her towards the cottages. Lucy cast a backward glance over her shoulder. She saw a man at Headquarters, in a straw hat and navy coat. He looked an awful lot like Massa Hendricks talking to a staff sergeant. Both women ran. Lucy felt the sermon's words take wing from her heart, replaced by a heavy weight of darkness. She stood to lose her new life possibly any minute.

When they reached cottage #8, Mama told Miss Fair, who promptly went for Narciss. Mama took Lucy's hand and said, "Miss Fair said go to the latrines. Wait it out there until she comes for us."

While inside the women's privy, Lucy clung to Mama's hand. Her heartbeats were a loud pounding within Lucy. Miss Fair popped in, "Ladies, Narciss is hidden. I'm going to Quartermaster Hall. Don't worry. We'll chase him off."

"Wonder what took him so long to come for us?" Mama asked. Lucy didn't answer. Perhaps he was only after his field hands or Rudy. Lucy sank down on her heels. She looked over at Mama in the dim light. Her eyes were squeezed shut and her lips quivered. She was praying. Lucy followed suit but it was a repetitive prayer, her fear robbing her of mental reasoning.

Thirty minutes elapsed. Miss Fair suddenly appeared, with Narciss in tow. "It's alright, ladies." She sank on the dry sand beside them. "Quartermaster Hall got rid of him." She caught her breath.

Mama ventured the question, "We're safe now, you think?"

Miss Melinda Fair suddenly beamed her smile. "You have no reason to fear. Quartermaster Hall never told him you were here and wouldn't allow him a search."

"Why not?" Lucy asked, "I've seen other masters looking for their slaves. Massa was here before and got Rudy."

"Well, I don't think Quartermaster Hall particularly likes the man. And Mr. Hendricks wouldn't admit to supporting our Union army. If he were loyal to the Union, Quartermaster Hall would be obligated to aid him in finding his lost property. But your master is a man of principle. He skirted swearing allegiance to our cause, so Quartermaster Hall wasn't under any obligation to help him." She smiled wryly.

Mama snorted, "Man of principle?"

Miss Fair laughed, then said, "But I suspect Theron Hall wouldn't have helped him anyway, loyalty or not. He didn't the other times."

She noted the women's surprised looks. She nodded, "Yes, he's thwarted your master before. He's rather fond of you, ladies. I think he's never had such sharply pressed shirts, like you can do, Angelina. His superiors comment on how orderly he appears. That's no small feat in the army." Then she blushed and stood, brushing off her skirt.

They all suddenly laughed, their tension evaporating. Narciss put in, "Guess we can get out of here now." Noticing where they were brought more laughter.

Mama quipped, "Guess hiding out in the privy has taken on a whole new meaning."

The jolly group of women emerged from the outhouses, earning them a stare and headshake from a young corporal passing by. Lucy's joy felt unchecked. All in one day, she had heard and seen manifested, the Words of life.

Chapter 11

Independence and Sacrifice

"Well, would you look at that!" Narcissa, on her way to the kitchen, had stopped abruptly, causing Lucy to plow into the back of her.

"At what?" Lucy peered over her sister's shoulder. Groups of men milled around in the semi-darkness. In the east, a faint hover of pinkish light, tinged with orange, became evident along the skyline. It cast enough light to make the figures discernable. They were soldiers, dressed in blue uniforms, and they were black.

Lucy's eyebrows rose. "I know they said they'd be enlisting, but I didn't believe it."

Just a week ago, Miss Fair had brought the good news. Kentucky would enlist black men to bear arms for the nation. She had been so excited. There was so much to do, she claimed.

Reverend Fee had great plans for these men. Teaching was paramount, not only the scriptures, but reading and writing. The American Missionary Association was going to be in their element, Miss Fair had beamed.

It had been the truth. Miss Fair might have more work ahead of her, but so did Lucy and Narciss. When they reached the kitchen, Cook Sam was slamming around the pots and skillets. Two other cooks were also on duty.

Mama came barreling through the kitchen, from the mess hall. Sam glared at her. "You tell them idiots breakfast ain't gonna be on time?"

Mama nodded, "I told them that. But," she soothed, "I reckon with extra help, we'll manage." She turned to her girls. "I'm finding more help to serve. You girls work in here."

Cook Sam continued his spiel. "They wake me up at 3:00 a.m. this morning. Tell me I got 254 more recruits to cook for. Ain't that like the army? Get themselves some more men and all but forget they got to feed 'em! 'Oh, we'll let Sam work it out. He can do anything in the kitchen.'" He mimicked some official, jabbing a wicked knife while he cut off rashers of bacon.

Lucy wanted to laugh, but she was fighting her own battle with the bacon that was stuck to the cast-iron skillets. Once it was all turned, her mind wandered to this sudden change and what it might mean.

In the summer of 1864, Kentucky's long-held restrictions against arming their black men were lifted. No longer was Kentucky allowed to be a colicky baby, held by an attentive mama. The government would no longer rock her soothingly. Kentucky's governor, Thomas Bramlette, among others, was forced to enroll any black man who would volunteer his services.

The human stampede was under way. Unrestrained, 574 black men enlisted immediately at Camp Nelson. By July, 1,370 strove to register their loyalties and by September, another 1,199 added their names to the roster. At the war's end, which came nearly a year later in April 1865, 5,405 slaves had become members of the United States Army.

Lucy was wide-eyed at the changes, which crept upon her like bread dough rising. One hour it lay all flat, and next it had swelled to nearly double. If the camp had seemed busy as ants before to Lucy, it now resembled a hive of bees in full production. The noise levels increased along with the activity. Suddenly, the women of cottage #8 were awake long before the sun was, and went full-throttle until the moon rose. Lucy would wearily pull off her stockings and tumble onto her cot, wincing at her protesting muscles as they settled down to cease motion. Then by morning, her adrenaline was recharged and she plowed into another day.

Sometimes the morning dishes were scarcely done, when lunch was already in full swing. But she would be off to wash uniforms and press shirts before the final meal at 6:00 p.m.

Reverend Fee had opened several schools to teach letters and sums to the new recruits. Miss Fair had told Lucy if she had spare time, come down to the school between classes and see what she could learn. She had whispered, "A knowledgeable woman is an independent woman". Lucy had smiled politely but wondered lamely what "independent" meant. It sounded more like a painful ailment to Lucy, who needed no extra impediments.

Now the camp had swelled its perimeters with women and children who had followed their men to the army. When the cottages became full, tents and shacks were built along the camp's gates. When black slaves went to enlist, they often left behind their wives and families, who were subject to the master's displeasure and disapproval.

Lucy heard story upon story of beatings and cruelties until she dreamed of them. But sometimes it was no dream when she listened to the cries of women being reclaimed by their master and dragged back to their former homes. Lucy wept with them or stuffed her head under her pillow to muffle the sounds.

*　　　　　　*　　　　　　*

One day Lucy helped Reverend Fee between classes, along with Miss Fair. She collected the primers off benches and stacked them neatly on a table. She was too busy to attend the women and children's class yet, but already she had picked up the alphabet by listening. She could recognize several letters. She was doing what Miss Fair suggested.

Rev. Fee smiled at Lucy. "You get an A for diligence, Lucy. When are you going to come *for* class, instead of coming to clean up *after* class?"

Lucy smiled back but shrugged. "There's an awful lot of work to do now."

Rev. Fee's smile disappeared. He sighed. "The army is not too happy about the situation. Our hands are full, trying to better the recruits and care for their families' needs. But the government owes it to them." He tossed a ruler on the desktop where it clattered. Miss Fair jumped. Seeing Rev. Fee's serious expression, she turned and took a seat to listen better.

He continued, "It's all a testing ground. But it will be proved, I'm sure of it."

"What will be proved, Rev. Fee?" Lucy questioned.

"The ability of your people, Lucy. They are as capable as white men, maybe more so. Their families deserve fair treatment and the army needs to supply for their needs. So far it has been a terrible tug of war."

Lucy had seen that. Masters tugging on their property, women tugging on their children, husbands and wives tugging not to be torn apart.

Rev. Fee pulled his pocket watch from his vest pocket. "Oh, I'm late. I had a meeting with General S.S. Fry. Excuse me, ladies." He hurried off.

Yes, Lucy thought, Rev. Fee was tugging on army officials for more food and better treatment, along with the Lord for His divine intervention as well.

Miss Fair sighed. "Well, the wheels are rolling now. From here to the war's end, we'll see change like none other, despite any opposition. You can't stop a runaway wagon going down-hill, can you?" She seemed pleased with the notion.

Lucy finished her task. When the last slate was set in its place, she turned to Miss Fair.

"I'm happy for our people. But there's a lot of misery outside the camp's gates. I don't think the army cares. I know Kentucky doesn't care. Who does care?"

Miss Fair drew in a sharp breath. "God cares. The American Missionary Association cares. Rev. Fee cares. I care. You –."

Lucy interrupted her diatribe. "What I mean is, there's going to be a lot more suffering. What happens when those men get killed? Their wives aren't going to be any better off." Lucy trusted Miss Fair, who had taken on a great responsibility. She marshaled cottage #8 admirably. She aided Rev. Fee's schools and church services, all the while advancing the A.M.A.'s cause. Lucy realized they were near in age and slowly the conventional gap had closed. They worked together and shared a common goal, growing close to one another. Lucy was in awe of her. Now she waited for Melinda Fair's sentiments.

Miss Fair sat still. She tilted her head then and spoke slowly. "There is always much pain in change. It takes sacrifice on someone's part but in the future …. Well, it is usually worth it. I happen to know a little about it."

Lucy was interested. She settled herself on a bench, facing Miss Fair, waiting for her to continue.

"My father was a white businessman. He lived in New York where my mother was a servant in his household. She wasn't a slave, but nearly the same. There were and still are very few opportunities for a black woman, in the North or the South, as you know. Her people had run from Maryland and been living free in New York for twenty years.

"Anyhow, when my brother, Benjamin, was born, he looked pretty nearly white and my father had no heir, so he and his white wife took Benjamin to raise as their son. It broke my mother's heart to give her son up to this white woman, but she did. Then I came along. The white wife wasn't very happy. I looked black except for my green eyes. She talked her husband into selling us to the fugitive slave catchers, just as if we had been slaves. My mother had no papers to prove otherwise. So although we were on northern soil, my father sold us back to slavery.

"But on the train south, my mother broke free of the trackers with me in her arms and ran. She ran all over that station and out into the city until she lost her pursuers and ended up in the gutters. A drunkard took her to the city's missions, which happened to be the A.M.A., the American Missionary Association. She was able to find work again, but not with me. A white couple offered to keep me in their household and I grew up there, cared for well, but a servant nonetheless. I did get schooling, along with their children, but I waited on their table and sewed their clothes."

Here Miss Fair paused. She had a faraway look in her eyes; their green tint took on a shiny quality.

"My mother made the best of what she was offered. She wanted better for her children. She sacrificed for my brother, gave him up to be raised white, because it would be best for him. She sacrificed herself to flee from those traders to save us. She sacrificed for me, letting me be raised by those white missionary people, to better my life.

"So, here I am. The A.M.A. gave to me long ago. Now I give to it, serving where I can. I decided as a little girl to be independent and serve God in any capacity. And I've learned that all worthwhile things take time and sacrifice."

Lucy wiped her own eyes. She asked quietly, "Where is your mama now?"

"In Heaven," came the quick reply. The sober face reflected grief for a moment, and then it gently changed, to send forth its beam. Lucy saw all the courage Miss Fair possessed in that smile. Miss Fair stood and gripped Lucy's forearms sisterly. Her voice was a whisper. "Things are what you make them."

Then she left Lucy, who long stared after her as if she had just seen the whole course of history change before her eyes. All from Miss Melinda Fair's brave smile.

*　　　　　　　*　　　　　　　*

When Lucy lay awake in bed that night, she watched the shadows on the walls. They were alive with Miss Fair's story. Lucy studied the shadows. They were black and white. Was everything under the influence of those two colors?

What was required of her? What sacrifice would she eventually make, if any? She wondered about the word independence. Rev. Fee told her it meant freedom. She could understand that. Would it be painful, she had asked him? Lucy could picture his patient, kind face looking thoughtful. "Yes, it sometimes is." Miss Fair had also said that change was painful.

As Lucy listened to the familiar camp sounds in the night–horses stomping, a mule braying, a stray dog howling and the sentry giving watch–she realized a great thing. Change was coming, like one of those miraculous, fancy steam engines on its tracks, purposefully charging toward its destination.

Sometimes change stole from people, but sometimes it could be generous and bestow gifts. Regardless, it was always many-faceted, like any worthy jewel. There was great opportunity ahead, but it had a price. As the shadows deepened and Lucy tossed one final time, she realized the price of change was often veiled–at the hidden core lay personal sacrifice. And Lucy would not be exempt.

Chapter 12
Allen

Lucy was sent to fetch water Monday morning. The day was sporting blue skies and the heat had not yet risen to embrace her. As she walked along, she contentedly mused on what she liked so much about her new life. When she reasoned it was the work, she was nearly stopped in her tracks by the irony of it all. Work was the very thing she had despised in her former existence; the difference being she no longer toiled in servitude for no gain. Here the Camp teemed with activity and excitement, providing respite from the labor, and all toward a worthwhile end.

Another difference was the noise level. Clover Hill had always been so quiet, and so had Redmond to a certain degree. As Lucy paused and listened, there was a multitude of sounds that emanated from camp life, none of them terribly disagreeable. Her ears came to accept the horses and mules' brays and neighs. Steam hissing in arcs toward heaven no longer startled her. Alternately, the clanking metal and groaning wood seemed like a daytime lullaby. Once, Lucy had thrilled to the bugle's call of reveille, now it was as standard to her ears as the dominating sound of men's voices: the watch called in tenor, military orders in baritone, and curses in bass. It all blended together until Lucy was fully immersed within it and a part of the sounds. Now, there were new sounds for her ears to hone in on: babies crying and women's voices always calling or scolding. Somehow this commotion disturbed the peaceful, audible clamor of before. It reminded her of adding one last hoecake to the pile and toppling the stack right off the platter. It made Lucy wince.

It was the sounds of the times though. Lucy wished all the women could be working joyfully like she was, no fear of uncertainty. But they had children to tote and resourceful work was becoming limited. There would be more expulsions, she was sure.

She shook her head to clear the disturbing thoughts. They would not cloud the happiness she felt today. Camp Nelson was an exciting place. This was the place beyond the hills she used to wonder about as a little girl. There was praise in her heart and a song on her lips when she reached the pump house.

"Look at that smile, fellas. You come to brighten up our day, little lady?"

Lucy was suddenly in the midst of the water detail. She sobered. "I was to tell you we need some water hauled to cottage #8 for the washing. But I need this bucket filled too." She held it out and four hands reached for it simultaneously. Then one hand more appeared and grasped it atop the others, pulling it out of their reach.

"Come on, now." The voice reminded Lucy of a stone dropping to the bottom of a well, and the deep reverberations that followed. "Start hauling water. That's what you're paid for." The young man, who owned the voice and the upper hand, took the bucket, and motioned Lucy over to a steel vat pumped full. There were protests from the other men, but he waved them off, mumbling under his breath.

Lucy followed. She eyed the stranger curiously. He was a lot taller than she was, which was nothing new, but there was an aura around him, one that made the other men mind him. *Interesting.*

He barely looked at her while he talked. "Who sent you down here for water?"

"Sergeant Ribford. Why?"

He scooped the bucket full and set it down, looking directly at her for the first time. "'Cause you really need to send someone less likely to distract the men from their work."

"Hmm. Like who? I always drew and carried my own water before. Anyhow, they're all soldiers up around the compound."

"You here on your own?"

"It isn't none of your business, but I'm here with my mama and sister."

"Well, send your mama then."

"You ain't never seen my mama."

He looked hard at her to see if there was any banter in her tone, but finding none, snatched up the bucket. "I'll carry this back for you while the men get water pumped to #8." He strode off briskly. Lucy had to hurry to catch up. The workmen shouted catcalls at them.

He looked at her sidewise, "See what I mean?"

"Well, it wasn't my fault. I'm doing like Sarge said."

"Yeah, well, it's my job to see the men stay on task. We're workin' here, and we're out to prove something. I can't have them getting off course."

Lucy found this young man strange. She had never met one so reserved, yet mixed with straightforwardness. "What are you out to prove?" She couldn't resist asking.

He stopped, "That we're just as able as the white men here in this camp."

Lucy was puzzled, "Why you need to do that? They're already enlisting our men."

"That don't mean nothin'. You think they think we're all equal?"

Lucy hesitated, "Well, that change is going to take some time."

67

He set the bucket down in the dusty street. A mule driver with his team passed, watching them with curiosity. When the dust cleared, Lucy found the young man studying her, frowning. "I don't have that much time. I'm guessing you've been taught from a baby not to question anything."

Lucy's brows rose. Her mama had failed her for sure. Amused, she laughed, "Oh, my mama said my questions were like poison sumac on a hot day!"

The man's face softened. "You going to the school they got here?"

"Not yet, but I want to learn sometime."

"And why's that?" He was direct. Lucy fumbled for an answer. That was always harder than asking the question.

"Well, because it's …." She wasn't sure how to put her feelings into words. "It's something better. It's independence."

He nodded, understanding. "Right. You need learning. When you wash and cook and can read and write, then you ask yourself if you're any different from a white woman."

Lucy stared at him as if he had just suggested the order of the universe was all wrong, as if the moon didn't follow the sun, or the bees didn't like flowers.

"Don't look like that. You're free now, ain't you?"

"I guess… from Massa Hendricks anyhow. Massa Charles may still own me." Lucy was suddenly confused.

He noted her bewildered expression. He picked up the bucket and said, "You need to learn to think like a free woman. You learn what Mr. Fee's teaching. You'll get the idea."

Lucy narrowed her eyes at him. He looked away from her. "Come on." He reached #8 before she did and deposited the bucket on the wooden steps. Several women leaned out the windows of the stilted building. Little children stared, their thumbs stuck in their mouths.

Ignoring them, he asked, "What's your name?"

"Lucy."

"Lucy what?"

"Just Lucy," she answered, suddenly embarrassed.

"Well, Miss Lucy, you need any help, ask Capt. Hall about

me. Name's Allen Ross. I'm usually about on some detail or another around here." He turned abruptly and left.

Lucy took the water into the cottage amid staring eyes.

At the south wall, she poured it into the pitcher on the washstand. She did not look up until Narciss appeared. "So that's what took you so long," she teased gently.

Lucy blushed but met her sister's eyes. "It weren't nothing. You know that."

Narciss nodded and followed her out to the washtubs. Mama was organizing the filling of the vats and heating water in the immense kettles over the fire.

As Lucy pitched in, she kept pondering on one train of thought: *how does a free, independent woman act?*

✳   ✳   ✳

When the lessons ended, Lucy gathered the primers and slates and stacked them nicely. She moved between the benches, looking for an excuse to linger. She watched John Fee out of the corner of her eye, manufacturing the courage to speak to him. Unfortunately, it was taking its own languid time coming about.

Finally, the kind voice came across the open space of the schoolroom. "Lucy, child, all that is left would be to varnish the floorboards since you're wearing out a path between the benches. Come here."

Lucy obediently went to Mr. Fee's desk. He smiled at her and waited patiently until she looked up. "What's troubling you?"

Lucy was horrified when she blurted out, "Rev. Fee, how does a free person act?"

He did not smile and a furrow appeared on his brow. "Let's see. What does being free mean first of all?" He spoke like he was asking himself the question. "Here's our trusty dictionary." He pulled the volume from a pile precariously stacked on his desk.

He paged through until he read aloud, "'Enjoying personal

freedom: not subject to the control or domination of another. Capable of choosing for oneself.'" He read quietly for a moment, then snapped the book shut. "What do you think of that?"

Lucy drew a breath. "It sounds wonderful, yet frightening too."

John Fee nodded, "Exactly. Freedom is wonderful but you know it isn't without a price. Simply put, Lucy, it's a big responsibility." He asked quietly, "Are you up to it?"

"I don't know, sir. I've always been so busy working for Massa, yet it's always been a part of me, wantin' to be free. I'm worried about the future. Worried I won't know how to act."

He smiled and tapped a finger against his books. "I think you have all the capabilities of a free person. It's all there inside you. God made it so. This nation has taken the hard way around to achieve what will eventually come. If men would have only followed their God-given instincts, they could have avoided this bloodshed. But I'm convinced it must be, to bring the nation to its senses. You keep on learning, Lucy, and it will come to you. I'm here to help."

Lucy thought of something else. "Am I going to have to talk to Massa Hendricks to see if I'm free?"

John Fee shook his head. "Consider yourself free now. We'll protect you. Our side is slowly winning and the war will end. Before long, all your people will be able to claim their God-given rights. You needn't fear."

"And if your side doesn't win?" Lucy clenched her hands together nervously.

"Oh, but we will. Right always prevails. Now rest your mind. You have cleaned up sufficiently and you can be dismissed. I have another class of soldiers due any minute."

Lucy was relieved. In awe of Mr. Fee, she could only swallow hard and nod, as she absented the schoolhouse. She was sure she would never gaze on another angel in the flesh as true as Mr. John G. Fee.

Chapter 13

August 1864

Misunderstanding

In the month that followed, Lucy ran into Allen Ross numerous times. Narciss suggested she take notice. Lucy certainly did notice, but not in the manner her sister meant.She found this new friendship so attractive, not because the man was, but because the conversation was. Allen set the universe in perspective for her. They talked about the many important things of life, things Lucy was just coming to understand. Lucy loved best when she discovered satisfying answers to her many questions with him. It gave her a fledgling feeling of control over life.

Lucy wasn't interested in romance, like Narciss. Life was real and life was earnest and marriage certainly was not her goal. Besides, Mama always had a good reason to shy away from certain things, especially ones in regard to men.

Sometimes while they talked, Allen would mention his

dreams. Lucy could understand them. They weren't of grand occupations or great scholarly learning. They were simple yet glorious plans.

"I want my own place that no one can take from me–my own family that can't be torn apart. Food for my table, clothes on my back and no man to call me to task. Now that's real freedom and peace."

Allen paused, "Right now, Lucy, I don't have that peace inside." Lucy listened intently. When Allen was serious, which was a good part of the time, Lucy hung on every word.

One night, while the crickets serenaded the night and the campfires glowed like tigers' eyes across the dark compound, Lucy sat beside Allen, her legs drawn up in her skirts, listening to the insects' song. Allen spoke to her profile. "I'm tired of the work detail. I've been here a year and this is all it's gonna be. The army's too busy to take notice how efficient we all work. I'm just good for hauling rock or water and digging a trench. I don't feel like I'm going anywhere. It's time for a little growth."

Lucy pondered his words. "Well, someone is needed for those things. They're important too. The others have up and enlisted."

"That's just it. Those jobs are important for what? So the camp runs smoothly for some white general? So we win this war? What exactly are they fighting for? What's my duty? If I enlist, is it just another form of bondage? This would have to be my war for me to join."

Lucy's mind swirled like the Kentucky River against its limestone walls. This was a very real aspect to consider. Where did the black slave fall into the scheme of things?

Allen continued, "We fight and win our freedom, and it'd be a great thing. But if it's just for another form of bondage, I don't know if it's what I want. What's the right thing to do?"

Lucy spoke quietly. "There may not be much choice for a black man. Have you talked to Rev. Fee about it?"

Allen tossed a stick into the fire. He put his hands on the top of his bent knees. "He said the war had to come about for this purpose. When they enlist men as men, not just white or colored, and we all work toward a common cause, the yoke of oppression broken, then things will change. My dream might have a chance of fruition."

Lucy tucked her skirts more tightly around her. She shivered as she watched the embers glow, barely feeling the faint warmth they radiated. "Allen, Rev. Fee said all good things take time. So will change. Our men can enlist now and fight for their freedom, real freedom. We have to believe in the good. We're better off here then we all were a year ago. Things may never be what we want, but we have got to keep moving forward. It takes faith, Rev. Fee said. I'm not going back to Massa Hendricks ever. So I've got a future. You, too, whether you work in the camp or enlist in the army. But we are going to have to sacrifice for the future, for something better. We can't be selfish."

Allen was quiet, digesting Lucy's words. He turned toward her. "Lucy, there's something else." His voice sank lower. "I'm afraid."

"You're afraid to fight?" Lucy asked, concerned as well as surprised.

Allen nodded. He gazed through the smoke, toward the black night. "But not like you think." Lucy waited, tense, until he continued. "Any man who's seen another man killed bare-handed or had his kin starved off in the woods or his baby sister abused–." He paused and swallowed. His head hung low.

"Well, he isn't afraid of war. I'm afraid of myself. Deep inside here." He tapped his chest. "I fear the hatred I've got buried. If I had a gun and free reign to kill, well, those white–. I'd lose myself for sure, and step over the boundary of what's decent." He heaved a great breath.

Lucy's eyes had grown wide. She rested her head on her knees and closed her eyes. Her muffled voice spoke, "You haven't forgiven, then, have you?"

"No." Allen struggled to regain his composure. His eyes flashed. "Can you?" Lucy didn't answer, but looked up into his dark eyes, which reflected the red embers. He continued, "It's going to take years, and then some. There are things you can't just say a prayer over and go on."

Lucy struggled inside. Did she really understand forgiveness herself? It sounded so heavenly, the peace and freedom forgiveness brought, especially the way Rev. Fee explained it.

"I don't want to go to that place inside of me. It's all that separates me from that man who called himself my master. If I go there, I'm lost. I'll never be any better than he is."

Lucy felt tears moving down her cheeks. Just then, she heard Mama call to her. It was curfew. "Oh, Allen!" Lucy could find no other words for her earnest friend. Distressed, she rose and retreated into the darkness. Her heart felt as bleak as the night. More questions with no answers.

The next time Lucy saw Allen, he took her by the elbow and led her over to the corrals. He seemed excited. Lucy looked at him questioningly.

"Lucy, it's taken me a while to work things out, but I'm going to do it. I'm going to enlist." He waited for her to respond. When she didn't, he pressed on. "Rev. Fee helped me unscramble my thoughts. But you were the one who really helped me reason it out. I think I'm ready to meet the future head-on."

A nosy mule pushed his nose through the rail fence. He nipped at Allen. Allen shoved his head back gently.

Lucy spoke, "I'm glad for you, Allen." Her words sounded hollow to her own ears. She was glad, wasn't she? "Being uncertain is a lost feeling." *Wonder if I've just lost my friend?*

"And," he continued, "I figured out I'm going to have to stay away."

Here's my turn to be unselfish! Lucy spoke woodenly, "You're going away? Already?"

"No, just stay away from you." He looked suddenly shy. "We have such good conversations, but I want to leave it at that. I see all these fellas juggling their service and a family, and I don't want a woman holding me down. I'm thankful I'm a bachelor. I want to keep it that way. Do you know what

74

I'm saying?"

Lucy's mind did a little footwork. She concluded that Allen Ross was being much too presumptuous to suit her. *Just like a man!* Aloud, she said, "What makes you think I enjoy our talks any more than you do? You're assuming an awful lot."

The mule brayed at Lucy. She slapped it. Surprised, it reeled backwards.

"Lucy." Allen looked pained. "I didn't mean to make you mad. I thought you would understand."

Lucy did not understand, neither him nor herself. She angrily swiped a strand of hair back under her kerchief. "Fine. You stay away. I've had lots of good talks with my washboard. Now you can try it with your bedroll."

Allen's lips were a fine line. He paused, then shrugged and walked away. Lucy watched his back until he disappeared in the mass of moving men. She looked at the corrals. Slowly her anger dissipated to a starched hurt. The mule came up and brayed once more at Lucy. It barred its teeth reproachfully.

That's right, you dumb critter! You go on and behave that way.

In Lucy's mind, at that moment, there wasn't much difference between men or mules or the way they acted!

Chapter 14

September 1864

Friendship

Miss Fair was weeping. Lucy stood, transfixed in the doorway, unable to decide if she should approach her. Then her inner urging carried her forward, and she trod softly to the bed upon which Miss Fair sat, her slender shoulders shaking, while her hands covered her face.

"Miss Fair?" Lucy asked tentatively. Miss Fair's head came up, and she hastily pulled a handkerchief from her dress pocket to wipe her glistening face.

"Oh, Lucy, I'm having a weak moment." She attempted a paltry smile. Lucy sat on the cot beside her. Most of the inhabitants of the cottage were asleep or outside, loitering in the dusty thoroughfare. They were as close as they could come to being alone.

"What's wrong?" Lucy steeled herself. Miss Fair did not have "weak" moments.

Melinda Fair hesitated, and then read the determined look in

Lucy's eyes. She spoke quietly, "There will be another expulsion. The army is going to clean house. Anyone without a special permit is going to be driven beyond the gates. There are so many women and children here now. The army says it isn't prepared to feed them."

Lucy shrugged, "They'll drive them out and they'll creep back after a day or two, just like always. Don't fret yourself, Miss Fair."

"No!" Miss Fair raised her voice, "It won't be like before. It's going to be worse, much, much worse!"

Lucy spoke, "How do you know?"

"Because Theron said–I mean Captain Hall, told me. He fears for the refugees here. He's seen the commander's orders–." She broke off, and they both listened to the natural chorus outside the cottages.

Lucy broke the silence, "You work pretty close to Captain Hall. He tell you everything?"

Miss Fair looked as if Lucy had physically smacked her. She straightened up, her spine curving backward. Her lovely pecan color turned rosy. Lucy raised her eyebrows at the blush.

"Why Miss Fair! Captain Hall's old enough to be your daddy! And he's white!"

Melinda Fair was horrified. She jumped to her feet and scanned the cottage to see if anyone was listening. Her emerald eyes flashed.

"Lucy! First you show no compassion for the refugees and now you say such things to me? Don't you know my hand holds your pass to stay here?"

Now it was Lucy's turn to scramble to her feet. She blinked in surprise. She realized she had it coming about her coldness toward the expulsion orders. But they usually amounted to very little on the Army's part. As for her future in Miss Fair's hands, well, that may be true, but Lucy resented her friend's reference to it. Maybe they weren't as sisterly as Lucy believed.

Miss Fair took a deep breath and spoke calmly, but there was a tinge of iciness to her tone. "I have a lot of work to do now. I'll have to shuffle jobs and make lists of those needing permits. I'd better go see to it." She turned and slipped gracefully toward the door. Once there, she turned. "And Lucy, things aren't always what they seem." She left the cottage much as if in the wake of an Arctic ice floe upon a troubled sea.

Lucy bit her lip. Why, oh why, had she spoken out of turn? There was a dreadful feeling welling up within her innards and her heart felt as if it had touched a hot coal. Swallowing, she tried to relieve the painful pressure. Goodness! If Miss Fair wanted to fool herself...!

Then, as Lucy's more mature nature pressed to the fore, she had the grace to give up her defense. If Theron Hall was 43 years old, white, and married with a daughter near Miss Fair's age, it was no reason for Lucy to have opened her mouth. Miss Fair was accountable to no one but herself.

Standing in the unnaturally quiet room, as the military world moved on outside the windows, Lucy realized in dismay that she had just estranged herself from another friend. She exited the room and went out into the September sunlight to join the throng and press toward Rev. Fee's schoolhouse. As Miss Fair had said, things aren't always what they seem. A guilt-burdened Lucy moved on.

Fortunately for Lucy, she remembered the manners her mama had taught her and the training she had received at Redmond about entering a room. Very smoothly and quietly, she slipped in unnoticed. But even if she hadn't learned the etiquette of entry, her feet were fixed to the floorboards – the scene before her demanded such. Her backbone melted into the doorframe of the schoolhouse of its own accord.

Three men stood, embraced as a trio, in the center of the room. Lucy was not positive this was a friendly encounter until she saw them move apart, revealing a beaming Rev. Fee. The two other men, dressed in suits resembling preacher material, continued with the greetings. Lucy was mortified she had stumbled in upon them.

All three gentlemen noticed Lucy, and one came toward her. Lucy's eyes went wide. This man was black!

"Rev. Fee, we have a visitor." They all chuckled.

"Ah, Lucy. Come here and meet two of my associates. They have come to help with the great task ahead of us, schooling and ministering to our troops and the mass of humanity that sits at the gate." He looked grave and shook his head.

"We're glad to finally arrive." This was spoken by the white, portly gentleman. "Trains were on schedule and the roads were in good condition, especially out of Nicholasville." He swiped dust off his vest.

"Lucy, this is Rev. Abisha Schofield," Rev. Fee interjected. "He's a great part of the A.M.A. and has come to give us his aid."

Lucy tried to be polite and greet the identified man but her eyes continually strayed to the black man.

"And this is Rev. Gabriel Burdett. He ministered at the Forks of Dix River Baptist Church. He is very valuable to the AMA as a spiritual leader, and I consider him one of my dearest and closest friends. He wishes to enlist for armed service, in freeing our brethren in bondage."

Aha, he was a preacher! Lucy nodded, dumbfounded. *A real black preacher!* She had mumbled her greeting so now she tried to summon some form of etiquette toward the two men to redeem herself.

"Could I get your guests some refreshments, Rev. Fee?" Lucy forgot all about her earlier quest, and became interested in this new development at the camp.

"That would be very satisfactory." John Fee nodded in agreement.

Lucy went directly to the kitchen. Knowing what a job it would be to squire a tray of full cups across the compound, she retrieved a metal pitcher full of dark tea, and carried the cups wrapped around her fingers.

"What's that all about?" Sam scowled. Lucy smiled at the cook.

"Rev. Fee has company. Important company." Sam harrumphed. Lucy persisted. "A real live black preacher, Sam. You should see him."

Sam snorted, "Who says, him or you?" Lucy shook her head and left the grouchy cook. Sam would be glum if Abe Lincoln came to call.

When Lucy returned, the men had settled on benches, relaxing. Their carpetbags were strewn at their feet.

While Lucy poured the tea, the men resumed their discussion.

Rev. Fee asked quietly, "How's my college at Berea faring?"

Abisha Schofield spoke, "The same as when we corresponded last. There are no new developments nor will there be until this war is over. But, mayhap we can make up for lost time then."

John Fee nodded vigorously, "My fervent desire." He turned toward Gabriel Burdett. "Tell me of your plans, Gabriel."

"I want to join the army here. But I feel my foremost duty is to aid you in the schooling of the recruits. Furthering the A.M.A.'s mission to Christianize and teach my people comes before my own desires." Gabriel Burdett gulped down his tea and smiled absently at Lucy as she refilled his cup. His attention was drawn to Rev. Schofield, who spoke next.

"Speaking of the A.M.A.'s mission, I've heard Levi Coffin plans a visit. He wishes to establish his Western Freedmen's Aid Commission here. Not to sound territorial, but we may need to pressure our correspondence in New York. If we could secure more donations, there would be no competitive sprint here at Camp Nelson."

Rev. Fee was amused. "You do see clearly, and I have felt the same," he admitted. "But Levi Coffin is a good friend and capable of great support. We must think of our black friends. Achieving their goals is of utmost importance. Although," he asserted, "I don't especially wish for the camp to be under the W.F.A.C. Their administrative powers are often of an adverse nature."

"They frequently get the edge over the A.M.A. because they are more centrally located in Cincinnati." Rev. Schofield added.

Rev. Burdett agreed, "And it's no secret the food and clothing barrels are just as needed. They send more charity in that form and it is often more appealing to the masses than our words are."

Rev. Fee smiled. "That is rightly so. The miracle of the loaves and fishes proved many must be fed in a natural way before they can receive of the spiritual manna. It takes all our efforts. The Army, I'm afraid, does not want to shoulder their part. They don't want to be responsible for the soldiers' families. They cannot recognize that it would be a major draw for Kentucky's slaves to rise up and enlist if they knew their families would be cared for in some manner. In all, it's the Army's duty."

Abisha straightened his cramped legs and stood. He checked his watch and noticed Lucy sorting primers as if readying for lessons. Lucy appeared unmindful of them. He spoke, "You know, there would be such a concentrated effort on the part of the slaves to win their freedom, if only they could be free to do just that. It is the edge the Kentucky slaveholders still hold over them–even while the black men enlist and serve, their families suffer at the hands of the white masters."

"More than that," Gabriel Burdett finished, "In serving the government, we are not considered in the same capacity as a white man. And believe me, we've got more gunpowder for the spark than a host of Union northerners could ever have." He slapped his knee for emphasis.

Lucy had been busily minding the business of the three men, but working to appear as unobtrusive as she could. She knew something of the school in Berea that Rev. Fee had started nearly ten years earlier in 1855 where students both black and white could learn together. And of the A.M.A. and W.F.A.C. rivalry. Miss Fair had even explained who Levi Coffin was. She had said the Quaker man was an ardent abolitionist, who defied throngs of pro-slavers.

Now she listened intently as she gathered slates together. "I fear for the people, all the refugees, who have left their masters and came here for succor. I'm afraid until we can make Washington understand, they will keep turning them out in droves. Our hands are tied and it breaks my heart. We must keep returning good for evil."

The gentlemen decided to continue their discussion after Abisha and Gabriel had rested from their journey. Lucy offered to show them their quarters at the White House, where the officers stayed, on her way to the bakery where she was to help Mama bake bread that afternoon. Once she pointed out the building, she took her leave from them and popped in the back door of the bakery.

Mama had her hands in a large mixing bowl, flour up to her elbows and a dusting of it covering her face and hair. Lucy smiled. Mama did not. She narrowed her eyes at her offspring. "Where you been? You're late."

"Sorry, Mama. Guess who I met? A black preacher and another one who have come to help Rev. Fee."

Mama, of course, had nothing to say. Neither man had any bearing on whether she got the dough rising and another batch mixed up before the supper meal.

"Hop to it, Lucy." Mama ordered. "Grease them pans and make loaves. Hungry men are impatient men, and them kind of men want to boot your backside right out of this here camp."

Lucy suddenly remembered her early morning strife with Miss Fair. "Miss Fair been to see you, Mama?" she asked.

Mama slapped a loaf into a pan and grabbed another. Never breaking stride with her work, she sprinkled flour into a pan and grabbed more dough. "Yes, she's been here and gave me three passes to help keep us here, but she said she couldn't promise they would hold. Something about orders of complete restoration, whatever that means."

Lucy hesitated at her job. "Mama, I owe Miss Fair an apology. I spoke out of turn, something that was none of my business."

"Wouldn't be the first time, would it?" Mama gave her a scorching look. Lucy frowned.

"I feel real bad about it, Mama. Soon as I'm done here, I'm

gonna go make it right."

Mama did not speak until the loaves were covered and ready to rise. She sighed. "Miss Fair said she owes you one too. But I wondered. You make it right, Lucy, in case you ain't given another chance. No one knows the tomorrow, and we sure can't count on the butter 'fore it gets churned. Now go on, and meet me at the kitchen when you're done."

Lucy searched in all the places she felt Miss Fair might be. All except the privy, which she was sure would be an embarrassment and not the appropriate place for an apology.

Finally, Lucy knew she could spare no more time looking and started for the kitchen. On her way, she saw a youth on the ground, his back against the mess hall wall. His face was hidden by a book that rested on his knees. As Lucy paused to study him, he looked up.

"Hiya," he said. His elfin face was framed by unruly hair and a pair of spectacles were strapped across his face. There was a familiarity about him. He unwound a metal piece off each ear and folded them carefully. Then he pointed to his book. "Ever read *Gulliver's Travels* ?" When Lucy shook her head, he frowned. "Papa says I shouldn't waste my time, but–." He shrugged. " 'A boy needs to fan the flames of his mind' as my tutor used to say. I've already read the Bible through three times."

Lucy raised her eyebrows. The youth certainly seemed a scholar. "I'd sure like to read this much of the Bible." Lucy held her fingers two inches apart. "But I ain't got much time for schooling."

The boy smiled. "Haven't. You haven't got much time for schooling. That's how you say it. Listen, all I have is time. Could I teach you? Maybe stand beside you while you work and point out letters?"

Lucy stared at his hopeful face. She was doubtful. "You'd probably get chased out of the kitchen. Sam's kind of strict." At the crestfallen face, she added, "But we could try. I'd sure like to learn."

He stood. He was taller than Lucy was. She laughed. "How

old are you?"

"I'm fifteen." He was a gangly, white boy for his age. "I'll meet you at the kitchen tomorrow. I have to help Papa this afternoon."

He turned away hastily, remembering his duties. Lucy called after him. "What's your name?"

"Burritt Fee," he shouted.

Lucy smiled. Of course! She had heard of the boy. And after losing two friends, she was pleased to make a new one.

Chapter 15

September 1864

Departure

September was arrayed like a strutting peacock. The nice weather adorned Camp Nelson much as beautiful plumage and made her vain. The camp flaunted her magnificent growth, from a once fledgling camp of raw boards to a mature outlay of several hundred buildings that housed and trained thousands of soldiers for battle. And all of this under a golden sun that glorified the month of September. But the fair weather did little for Lucy's dilemma.

The words she carried in her heart towards an apology to Miss Fair seemed lodged there. When she finally came face to face with Miss Fair, she spilled the "I'm sorry" right off her tongue in a brusque manner, not at all like she had planned.

Miss Fair, ever gracious, accepted, but the warmth had evaporated. She did not return the gesture. Lucy became unsure how to retrieve their lost camaraderie.

While Lucy brooded over her wilted friendship, army

officials passed through the camp, evacuating women and children. It was indeed a more thorough expulsion. Lucy showed her pass in a tense silence, and the soldier continued on in disgust. It was not far from her mind of Herod's pursuit once long ago. She shivered.

Miss Fair had been right. Women and children were driven out, farther than before. These women were the wives of the very soldiers who donned blue and took an oath of loyalty there in the camp. Cottage #8 had empty beds, as did most of the other housing facilities. The makeshift shelters outside the gates were left forlorn, like ghosts with empty eyes. It became quiet, not just from their absence, but from ranks of subdued soldiers whose families they belonged to.

Lucy had not seen Allen for two weeks. She carried her anger during the day, but at night it slipped away like the sunset, and she lay on her cot, masked with hurt. The evenings were lonely without their fireside visits. She would never understand men, black or white. What drove them to behave in the manner they did?

Burritt Fee hung around the kitchen, spelling words aloud. Sometimes he wrote words in the steam created by the kitchen's cooking. Sam growled, but let him be. He was after all, a Fee. Narciss adored him and even Mama was gentle towards him. And Lucy learned.

Sometimes they went outside to the stretched tent that was attached to the kitchen, where the cooling tubs sat, and wrote words in the dirt. On one occasion, Allen walked by in uniform with his comrades on his way to the mess hall.

Burritt followed Lucy's eyes. He knew they weren't on the lesson. He waited until the men disappeared, then spoke, "That soldier helped me out last week. A couple of recruits got me to ride some ornery mule. He rescued me. He your beau?"

Lucy shook her head. "No. Once he was my friend, but not anymore."

"Really? How can you be friends one day and not the next?"

When someone thinks he's more than a friend, and isn't!

That's how! But Lucy only mumbled an answer, and Burritt let it rest. Instead, he pushed Lucy to spell the word "friend".

"F- r-e," Lucy began.

"Lucy, you forgot the 'i'." He instructed.

Lucy sat down in the dirt, brooding unladylike. "Burritt, I can't spell it, anymore than I can be one it seems. Let's quit for today. I'm tired of it anyhow."

Burritt's youthful face gave her a skeptical look. He stirred the dirt around with his stick. "Sure. But Lucy, I'm your friend—even if you never learn to spell it."

Lucy felt her face relax. She smiled. "Thanks. Now I've got potatoes to peel before Sam gets *unfriendly* with me." She hurried for the kitchen.

The review parade resembled a brilliant painting. Lucy stood on the compound's edge, among a slim crowd of women left in the camp. The men, in their ranks, were multi-colored ribbons of blue and black with gold accents, all of which gave them a jeweled quality. The sun danced, gilding the picture to perfection. Beneath this cloudless blue sky, the officers rode white horses or satiny browns that stepped in tune with the marching men.

Ten companies, the 5th and 6th U.S. Colored Cavalry, along with the 123rd and 124th Colored Infantry stood in formation. Flanking the squads of men, the 12th U.S. Colored Heavy Artillery lined up and stood at attention before General Burbridge and General S.S. Fry. They paused for inspection; a lone drum beat rolling across the parade ground. Word whispered that there was an upcoming engagement in Virginia with the enemy. Once more the soldiers marched around, bearing arms and making quite a spectacle of themselves.

Narciss sighed, "Almost makes a woman fall in love, just looking at those uniforms."

Lucy rolled her eyes. "There's men in those uniforms, don't forget."

"Oh, I'll think on that next time I'm washing them." Narciss quipped mischievously.

Lucy elbowed her. She fought the nauseating feeling that there might not be a next time for some of them.

Mama shushed the girls. Lucy noticed Miss Fair sandwiched between Narciss and her mother. Lucy wished she was standing arm-in-arm with Miss Fair, but a lukewarmness still prevailed between them.

The parade ended. From the stand where the generals sat, behind a podium, stood Rev. Fee. He offered a prayer, then another officer gave a speech. He concluded that the troops before him would show the necessary valor and courage it would take to force the enemy into submission. These men were the finest fighting force on North American soil and the land would note their unequalled conduct around the world. After his praise, the band started up in full tempo the familiar refrain:

"We'll rally 'round the flag, boys,
We'll rally once again,
Shouting the battle cry of freedom!"

When the last note died away, someone gave a throaty yell. To a prophetic "hurrah!", up into the emboldened cobalt sky flew a kepi hat. The sun's rays caught on the metal medallion of crossed arms that blazoned its front. Glints of light bounced off, showering false sparks above them. Lucy watched as another hat was thrown, then another, until it resembled a small flock in the air. It swelled to nearly a thousand slouch caps, raining down from the heavens. Flags waved, and the ranks raised a shout. Whistles rebounded off the compound, and the noise level progressed to a roar. Lucy felt mesmerized by the scene. Her eyes began to smart, stung by wayward tears. *Of all the times to cry! When had she gotten so soft?*

At departure time, Lucy purposely stayed away from the farewell social. She worked at the washtubs, for once absent of uniforms. She scrubbed a few white shirts, but mainly played in the soapsuds with indifference. She needed to escape her own plaguing questions. She did not want to honestly face her feelings or her mind. She completely ignored her heart.

Scuff, scuff, clank, and jingle. Lucy froze. Only a soldier made those sounds, and Lucy had heard plenty of it while here in Camp Nelson. The noise halted. Lucy raised her eyes above the tub's edge to fall on a pair of dusty black boots. Slowly she raised her eyes to the soldier's face. It was him, coming to say goodbye.

His eyes strayed to her bare arms, where below tightly rolled-up sleeves, soapsuds clung. He glanced away and took a deep breath, "You still mad at me?"

Lucy shook her head, "Not anymore."

"Good." He looked her over, realizing how much he had missed. "You're looking real pretty there, Lucy."

Lucy's expression did not waver. He pressed on, "I've been doing some thinking lately. And I decided I've been too hasty."

"How so?" she ventured.

"Well, I thought a woman would tie me down, but I see I was wrong. When I come back, I want someone waiting for me. Someone to care."

"So you picked me?" Her tone was sarcastic.

He swallowed. "Lucy, I'm trying to tell you I miss you."

She nodded an acknowledgement. He changed tactics. "How come you're not down at the Farewell? Your mama and sister are there."

"I don't like goodbyes," she said.

"It don't hurt none, to say goodbye. It gives memories."

Lucy kept quiet. *Not if we're dead*, she thought.

"Well, I'll be riding out before daybreak. I plan on conquering the South, setting our people free, and letting that U.S. flag fly over this whole land once again."

"Did you have to practice much?"

"For what? Being a soldier?"

"No, your speech. 'Cause if you did, the time might have been spent polishing your boots."

"I like a woman who's observant."

Lucy leaned over her tub. She grabbed a shirt and scrubbed on the collar. Allen stepped closer. "Lucy, I'd like you to wait on me. And I'd–I'd like you to kiss me goodbye."

"What!? I never even said I'd wait on you! Aren't you

being a little too hasty again?" She raised her eyebrows at him.

"Maybe. But some of the ladies at the Farewell had some for the men. Seems you would since you're not mad at me anymore."

Lucy folded her arms across her chest. "Ladies, huh? Well, you just get yourself on down there and get some of those free kisses. And as for the 'not-mad' part, I'm still undecided."

Allen's jaw set. "You love being contrary, don't you?"

"No, I don't. I just expect a friend to act like one. You dropped me, selfish-like, and now you want to just pick up where we never even left off." Her eyes glowered at him.

He had the grace to drop his. "You're right, Lucy. It's just I'm all mixed-up." His face reflected his misery.

He stepped closer, until the washtub was all that stood between them. "I'm excited and I'm scared. I miss you. I think I'm in love–."

Lucy's head shot up to search his face. His eyes were serious. She let hers trail to the buttons on his tunic. The gold buttons, emblazoned with an eagle, stamped proudly with the letters U.S., swam before her vision. She allowed them to momentarily blind her, refusing to meet his gaze.

"Lucy," he said softly. "I'd like to give you a last name."

When her eyes did meet his, she saw no teasing in them. Something warm and tender glowed there. Lucy swallowed.

He stepped back. He was quiet for a moment, then smiled. "If we were promised to each other, would you give me one?"

"One what?" Lucy had forgotten along what lines their conversation had railroaded.

"A kiss."

"No," Lucy snapped.

"And why not?" he asked, annoyed. "You are being contrary!" Silence. In a calmer voice, he pressed on, "What would it take for you to befriend me again? An apology? You have it. I'm sorry."

Lucy was exasperated. She grabbed the washboard and roughly drew a garment across it. Her emotions heaved like the wash water. She found herself saying, "If you win the war and don't get yourself killed, I'll give you one little peck when you get home. Now, you satisfied?"

He was grinning at her, from ear to ear. "Little lady, you've got yourself a deal. And I want you to think on that addition to your name. Alright?"

Lucy watched him tread backwards, away from her, down the thoroughfare. "Just memorizing the picture you make," he called.

Lucy suddenly felt herself laugh. What a picture *he* made! She relaxed for a few moments, to watch him, her heart pounding.

Then she sobered when he disappeared around the rows of whitewashed cabins. Fear and nervous unease assailed her. What a ridiculous bargain she had just made! Yet more disturbing, what if he did not come back to claim it? Lucy rubbed her eyes where hot tears pricked, unmindful of the soap she blindly rubbed in.

Chapter 16

September – October 1864

Camp Comrades

"Get your stinkin' knee out of my back," growled the usually deep-throated voice.

"Sorry, sorry!" a rather puny set of vocal cords returned. The exchange that had once seemed amusing was now a regular nighttime ritual. Allen came to expect it, and it no longer drew a smile. This was the norm for camp life. Four grown men sharing a tent meant for only two. Rations were hard and dry and tasteless. Riding, marching and drilling were both the work and entertainment, all rundled into one joyless wrap for the 5th and 6th Colored Cavalry.

Evening campfires were no longer the same as the ones at Camp Nelson. Around the fire pit sat three other residents, displaying masculine prowess at its best (and sometimes worst). The lack of a feminine presence was woeful to Allen. His memories of a serious, dark-eyed girl gave him pleasure as well as melancholy. His bedroll was a poor substitute; it neither smiled nor smelled good.

He turned to Blake Riley. The young man was near his age but that was where their similarities ended. Blake wore his hair long, letting it curl and mat around his ears. He sported a thin bandana around his upper forehead, claiming it kept his head clear. Allen wondered if the young man had Indian blood.

Blake smoothly scooped up twigs and braced the fire for the night. All his actions were that way, laced in ease. During drill, he reloaded his rifle with fluid motions, and wielded it like a part of his own anatomy. In battle, Allen suspected Blake would draw a bead and fire as naturally as he drew breath. But for Allen, he felt his own awkwardness with the cold metal.

Now Blake motioned to the tent, where the two bedfellows struggled to settle for the night. "Makes you glad those two get it out of their system before we have to join them." Allen smiled. He threw the poor-grade coffee, now cold, into the fire and pushed the tin cup alongside the greasy skillet.

"Reckon I'll turn in. Need to be fresh for that moronic drilling in the morning." Allen spoke dryly.

"Hey, it beats latrine duty. That's where ol' Sourface stuck me tomorrow, until I can follow 'exact' orders," Blake laughed. "How'd I know his feet were in the way?" He chuckled some more.

Allen grinned at the memory. Ol' Sourface was Sergeant Henley. Blake's comical two-step and about-face hadn't caused the Sergeant any mirth when Blake had done it on the toes of his freshly shined boots. There was no such thing as "funny" in the army. Of course, latrine and kitchen duty hadn't taken the starch out of Allen's tent mate. Not yet, anyhow.

Allen turned in for the night, finding his face against a cold canvas wall. He sighed. He had known the army was no clambake but bivouacking sure lacked the finesse of the old camp life. They were, of course, on their way to battle.

Eventually the orders would come. The assignment ahead brought coexistent reactions: Allen's skin tingled with anticipation, yet crawled with dread. The first fight of his army career held a significance beyond just any common battle. It marked his transition from subdued to subduer, from powerless to powerful. It was a heady thought. Then there was that specter of death, always haunting a soldier's mind, unreal and yet a very real possibility. He batted away the thought. It would interfere with a promised kiss that Allen fully intended to claim.

Another sigh. Anymore, Allen was beginning to feel that sleep was really just another stingy taskmaster in disguise.

The days lengthened and pressed forward on the calendar. The whole encampment grew restless, waiting on orders that traveled not with horses' feet but seemingly crawled along like worm segments. Even the horses seemed to mind. Most were poor horseflesh and easily rattled. They were accustomed to a life of drudgery, so carrying a rider was easy work, despite the mileage. Allen appreciated his own mount, but a few poor guys really had a time convincing their horse to keep going. They were war-weary. Some had leg problems. While the 6th U.S. Colored Cavalry awaited orders, everyone, including the horses, camped.

The monotonous drilling and marching were broken only by the evenings around a fire now that the weather had become uncooperative. Few men owned overcoats. The army had been negligent in outfitting the 5th and 6th Colored Cavalry. Yet most recruits did not complain nor voice any ungratefulness toward Uncle Sam. The men of Allen's regiment were better outfitted than they had ever been before, with their entire forms fully covered. Issued regimental clothing felt like golden raiment to the recipient U.S.C.C. They had braved the cold with a lot less.

While the whole camp awaited orders, Allen and his fellow soldiers became comrades in a detached sort of way.

Of their little group, Cyrus filled the unappointed position of cook. The large man, who donned a perpetual scowl, decided from the start he "wasn't eating no mule food." He unceremoniously took over the skillet. No one argued. His beefy arms and facade made arguments lean impressively in his favor.

They called him "Cy", and Allen decided not to learn too much about him—it was easier that way. He felt the same about Bucky Larson.

In truth, Bucky Larson had made it into the army by stuffing his coat and lowering his voice to the deepest timbre he could. The nineteen year old was a sapling who bent to the winds of other men's wills. His eager manner seemed to annoy anyone he came into contact with. He had been shuffled around until he fell into Allen's encampment. The three men there, who each possessed a solitary demeanor, simply ignored him. This arrangement suited them all, even Bucky, who had grown tired of sleeping alone on the cold ground.

Fortunately for Bucky, he had some redeeming qualities. He could be quiet when warranted, and he liked to start fires. He rose first at daybreak to gather the wood and light the kindling. Next, Cy would follow and start breakfast. Allen usually brought the water to the tent, and Blake made the coffee, such as it was.

They followed this routine with satisfaction, and were all comfortable with it. Their pleasant, estranged relationship would probably have continued so if Bucky hadn't gotten so excited over Cy's hand.

It had been a long day. The soldiers had worked hard to keep warm, often breaking out into a sweat. When they spilled back to their individual camps, they started fires or stirred up coals to dry off and prevent an evening chill.

Bucky had revived the fire. Allen stacked arms. then unbuttoned his coat and pulled up a block of wood to sit on. Cy ambled up, clutching something in his hands which he held protectively against his chest.

Blake, who was grinding coffee beans, eyed Cy's full hands. "Whatcha got there, Cy?"

Cy opened his fingers slightly. White orbs glowed like moon drops. Blake whistled, "You rob a henhouse?"

Cy bared the tips of his teeth, the closest he came to a smile. "Fella owed me a favor. He repaid it in these eggs from the sutler."

Bucky's joy bubbled over. "You ain't got to share 'em, Cy. But I ain't had eggs for a long time, mebbe 'fore Aunt Lindy took sick and Massa had to butcher all the chickens left."

Cy gave him a hard look and grunted. He moved closer to the fire and squatted. "Bucky, unload my hands and I'll get this here skillet hot."

Bucky rushed to obey, all the while chatting about chickens and Massa's dull knife and wayward feathers that he had swallowed. Blake rolled his eyes at Allen. Suddenly, Bucky grew quiet. His eyes grew wide and he tilted his head like a docile dog.

"Cy, what happened to you?" Bucky asked in a hushed voice. Cy looked hard at his hands as if he had forgotten what they looked like. He flipped them over and wiped them on his trousers.

Grabbing the skillet, he pushed it to the hottest part of the fire and shrugged. He raised his eyes to meet Allen and Blake's.

"Nothing more than a little cooking accident."

"How'd you do it?" Bucky pressed.

"Boy, don't you leave nothin' lay? You don't want to know."

Bucky was quiet for a moment, then ventured, "You sure must have been cooking real fancy. I never seen Aunt Lindy burn no picture on herself–."

"Fool boy, it ain't no picture. That's called a letter. Didn't you get no schooling at the camp?"

By now, Allen and Blake's attention was piqued and they gathered closer around the fire, forgetting the indifference that had existed among them. They, too, wanted to see Cy's palm.

Bucky shook his head. "I wasn't smart enough to learn. Why, only thing I was good at on Melrose plantation was hidin'. I hid for seventeen years on the place 'fore Massa find out about me. All on account of Aunt Lindy–."

Cy broke in, "Hand me those eggs now. I'm hungry." Allen was sorry to hear Bucky cut short. What other strange things might he say?

Soon they were feasting on the eggs and grease-softened hardtack with coffee. A few fellows approached, offering a game of cards. Usually only Cy played, but he declined.

Bucky patted his full stomach and said, "Cy, can you teach me how to cook as good as you?"

"Maybe. You make it through your first battle and I'll show you some pointers."

"Just so I don't burn myself like you did. I wouldn't want that on my hand. Did it hurt real bad?"

Cy scowled at the youth. "No. No, it didn't. I didn't feel one second of it."

"Why not? You got a pretty tough hide or what!" Bucky was looking admiringly at Cy.

"Yeah, I got a tough hide alright, but that ain't why it didn't hurt none. I never felt it 'cause I was too mad."

"I'd be mad too, iffen I burnt myself like you did."

Cy's temper rose a notch. "I didn't burn myself, you idiot. I said my hand looks that way 'cause of a cooking accident. But the accident wasn't mine. It was my massa's. He happened to get himself killed with a butcher knife. And me–well, I got me a letter M burned in my palm, for an example, and put in the hold." Cy was calm again and stared into the fire. Allen stirred restlessly. He had a feeling what the "M" stood for.

Blake spoke quietly, "Where I came from, you'd have been strung a mile high or whipped to death. Not just branded."

Cy nodded, "That was next. I was chained in the smoke-house, waiting on the sunrise. Then the Yanks came through. Freed us all, and never asked a question. Just set us all free, and I followed the Army, then joined up."

Blake looked away from Cy. "You must have had a lucky star somewhere."

Allen looked at Bucky. He was shaking his head, his expression as if he had lost a relative. "Poor Massa and you. You both had bad luck, didn't you?"

Cy only grunted. He spoke no more and moved off to the tent. Blake moved closer to Allen and spoke, "We all have some hidden past. Sounds like Bucky may have more of one than any of us." His lips quirked, amused. "'Course I don't know if I believe him."

Allen nodded and watched Bucky as he readied for the night. His thoughts stole to Lucy. He realized how little he knew about her. In turbulent times, it hardly seemed to matter. Thinking of Lucy, Allen warmed. She could have a secret like Cy's, and he wouldn't care a lick. No, the past had little bearing in these times.

Chapter 17

October 1864

Saltville

The orders came to march. Like smoke from a haystack set aflame, excitement rolled out of the men, tangible in the air. They scrambled to pack and load the supply wagons. Due to the nature of the assignment, all men were on foot, weaving their way south through Virginia, while their mounts were left to chomp and paw.

Bucky had not traveled far when he removed his boots and slung them over his already weighted knapsack. His feet modeled the chicken pox, so plenteous were the blisters. Allen tried to gaze at them dispassionately. Now was not the time to feel soft toward Bucky. But he did ask, "Where's your socks?"

"Oh," Bucky said, indifferently, "I loaned them to Steven. He cut his finger and needed something to stop the blood."

Allen said wryly, "Did he need both of them?"

"Well, no. But George had a cold and no hanky."

Allen was disgusted. He was sure the soldiers were up to foul play. No, he didn't want to grow soft toward Bucky–likely the poor fellow would end up killed anyway. But it made his jaw set to think of grown men funnin' poor Bucky.

When they stopped for the evening to camp, all four men were silent until they finished their supper of rations. Bucky ate his entire portion using his fingers. Blake raised his eyebrows at him while Allen wondered where Bucky had stowed his utensils. With their bellies full, they began to thaw a bit. Cy drifted off to a card game and Blake went on some errand. Allen watched Bucky work on polishing his boots with skillet grease until his mind left the fireside circle and brought Lucy's face before him. He watched her slap the mule and nearly laughed out loud, but checked himself just in time. He saw her earnest face say to him, "You want to just pick up where we never even left off!" Who said dark eyes were expressionless? Not Lucy's. A whole surge of emotions was conveyed there in obsidian darkness.

Allen had wanted to save himself heartache and figured he needed to stay away from her, to protect himself from any hurt. His heart had been hurt enough times. It hadn't seemed worth the risk. But then Lucy's caring face caught hold of him, and he knew it would be worth any risk to see those eyes glowing with happiness. What was life anyhow but a gamble? Especially now, since he had become a soldier. He wanted to hurry that fragile bud along, outright pull each petal open to reveal the beautiful flower. He didn't feel like he had time to nurture and admire it until it opened into a full-blown bloom. Then, he had been leaving; tomorrow he might face death. He wanted to feel what it was like to be cared for by someone. He wanted that empty cavity within his heart to be filled, and the heartache of loneliness to go away. It had been time to draw close to another human being, not pull away, like he had done in times past.

His thoughts were interrupted by Blake, who settled on a stump and shaved a piece of wood of its bark. Then he began to cut on the wood carefully, with an apt precision. Allen followed his movements for a while, then yawned and reached into his knapsack. Bucky followed Blake's hands as well, mesmerized as each shaving fell to the ground like an errant snowflake.

Allen stood up abruptly and threw a pair of spare socks at Bucky. Bucky looked up at him in surprise. "See you wear 'em tomorrow. And don't go giving them away. I'm just loaning them to you."

Bucky's smile haunted his sleep.

Word filtered through the ranks about the upcoming engagement. It left the men in a jovial mood to finally be in on some action. If they were a little loud with their humor and everyday routine, no one minded. It was a false bravado that buoyed them to the hour where they would face life or eternity.

That morning, Bucky took the wooden spoon Blake handed him with delight. His profuse thanks seemed to irritate Blake, who turned his back on him and tightened the tattered band around his head.

Later, as they filed in ranks, Allen told Blake, "That was a good thing you did for Bucky."

Blake returned grimly, "Yeah, you too. Least we could do for the kid before he meets his Maker."

It was a reminder of the next hours ahead, and Allen felt his jaw tighten as he swallowed.

The morning wore on, with birdsong punctuating the air, and the world appeared very normal. When a sudden volley of noisy metal flew over the marching divisions, the world suddenly shifted to chaos. Confusion reigned as troops halted and men took cover. Word came down the line to prepare for a skirmish. The infantry in the front columns attached bayonets. Regiments divided. The cavalry milled around, studying Clinch Mountain where repeated fire broke from the craggy rocks as Confederate defenders took potshots at the oncoming army. The conflict was short, and as they moved forward to march, Allen was not impressed. The 6th Cavalry had held the back ranks.

At Laurel Gap the same action was repeated. General Burbridge knew the game. Time was stretched by holding his men at bay. There would be a waiting army ahead, defending the salt works he was bent on destroying.

At dawn the next morning, Allen's spirits were decidedly low. A cold night with no fire, tents, or cooked food made war near and real.

Allen eyed the staff around General Burbridge's makeshift tent. One man squatted holding a map, while another balanced a sheaf of papers on one knee. The general dipped a pen in ink and spoke as he wrote, "October 2, 1864. Saltville, Virginia. Smyth County. Time: 7:10 AM."

Allen noticed a commotion. Bucky was bothering the color-bearer. Through the foggy, cold morning he saw the lanky figure with its accompanying high voice, reinforcing his suspicions. He came closer and overheard the color-bearer, who held the flagstaff, fuss at Bucky, "It's my duty. Only way I'm going to give it up is if my last breath is gone. So git!"

Bucky walked dejectedly away. He spotted Allen and came over. "Fella won't share the flag. You know, it belongs to the whole company."

Allen tried not to smile, "He's just doing his job. He's the one who's got to carry it. You got to do the fighting. Seems more important to me." Allen didn't mention the enemy always shot at the color-bearer. Fool job.

Bucky trailed around, mournful-like, until the bugle called them to formation and the march began.

When the battle commenced, it started in a series of charges. The Confederates held the high ground, having settled strategically along the high river bluff skirting the town of Saltville. Their defense held for several hours, but gradually Allen's regiment made ground, pushing the rebel's line back from Sander's Hill.

Now, Allen stood for mere seconds surveying the breastworks ahead. Before him, companies of men began to swarm Cedar Ridge. He was no longer in the rear but a part of the action. Carried along, he was in an unreal world, as the mass of men surged forward. At first contact with the rebels, he flinched at the roar of the guns. The noise was almost a living thing, a huge beast roaring in defiance of the puny men striving to over-come it. As they advanced, it seemed as if the clamor itself must be pushed back in front of them before they could make any progress. He told himself it was just sound, nothing to fear. Mostly, he minded the itchy uniform, and, although the day was bereft of sun, he felt the sweat trickle down his back. He regripped his gun with moist hands.

Then the bullets came raining down like hail. They pinged in and off the ground and rocks, and, later on, bodies. He ducked one way, then another, but knew it mattered little. As his feet rose higher upon the ridge, and he stumbled no longer over rough terrain, but forms of once-living men instead, he willed himself to cease thinking. This was no longer civilization where a person needed to think; he must only do.

Doing meant forward and up. Allen raised his eyes. He saw the white faces of the enemy gathered there, defending the ridge. Intermittent flashes of fire from gun barrels lit up the space above, and black powder floated in the air, interspersed with gray, cloudy smoke.

They had topped the rise.

And there, face-to-face, were the rebels–white men who had profited off the sweat of the slave's brow. The white men's pale faces were now blackened by smoke, and their eyes, reddened and full of surprise, glowered with an animalistic intensity.

A blond Confederate lunged toward Allen. The rebel car-ried only a knife, as wicked as the expression on his youthful face. Allen's mind reeled. This white Southerner was younger than he, possessed by hatred, ready to dispense Allen of his life. His mocking expression displayed the arrogance he had been bred with since a child. And what for? For this moment? To once again have control over a black man?

Allen's insides twisted and burnt like he had been branded. What made this rebel think he had any right to feel hatred? When had Allen's people ever done anything to him to earn such hostility?

The many years where dark pain and helplessness and even

107

shame had lain smothered, now reared up like an uncontrollable cavalry horse. He saw his sister's abuse on her tormented face, his brother stretched on a rack until his bones popped. Then his own dear mama, too busy as a mammy of the white children to be a mother to him. And sweet Lela, sold away.

Allen's face felt a mask of rage as he pulled his gun upward and aimed it at the yellow-haired white boy. And yet ... The youth crouched, knife still upheld. He saw Allen's hesitation and sure of himself, he laughed mockingly.

Allen roared, yet before his finger met the trigger, the boy crumpled from some wayward bullet. Allen turned away, numb from the surge that had just eclipsed him.

And then, in a stunted sense of time, the grappling with the rebels was over. Now Allen took a gulp of the sulfuric air and surveyed the scene. A rush of elation overcame him.

They had done it! They had rushed and broke the rebels' line and forced them to skedaddle on down to Saltville. The exultation was welling up within the men gathered on the ridge. They were no longer a bowed down people, but subduers, equal to the enemy. The victory belonged to them, the 6th U.S. C.C.

Allen drew great heaving breaths and his euphoria began to disintegrate. Gun smoke and sulfur brought reality barreling through his present façade. He looked around. Littering the ground were bodies, not all clothed in gray, but also in blue. The stench that met his nostrils was newly shed blood and death. Misery in its freshest form.

Allen quickly turned over the nearest prostrate blue figure. No one he knew; no one from his company. He hurried to check a few more for signs of recognition or life. Then he dashed down the ridge to join the rest of the ranks as they surged onward to aid the 5th Cavalry's charge.

The fire raged down the ridge with fury. Allen heard the shot whistle past. Grape and canister appeared to hover like a swarm of hot hornets. The man beside Allen screamed and Allen watched in horror, as suddenly, the soldier became faceless. Another man dropped before Allen. As he stumbled over him, the valiant fighter no longer possessed a head. It was as if the men were all puppets, with limbs gone askew–their strings broken.

As he neared the higher ground, Allen once again looked upward. The whole ridge wriggled like a live rattler, men swarming and recoiling. Explosions rocked the ground under his feet. The scene was of such fantastic horror; Allen could not have dreamed such a sight in the vilest of nightmares. The white Confederates were infuriated that men once under their subjugation, dared scale the ridge and offer fight. Their hatred and savagery could have killed, second only to ammunition.

Lieutenant Colonel Robert Ratliff's brigade, comprised of Allen's companions, strove to overtake, only to have their ranks repulsed. Dead men made barriers for the next surge to over-come. Again they charged up the ridge, Allen struggling with the rest. Heaving with great effort, he used his hands in sheer desperation to gain a hold, while he strove not to lose his rifle. Up and over was his only thought, like a mantra giving him momentum, wondering when a bullet would end this madness.

Allen swiped a grimy hand over his eyes to clear the sting from them. They had topped the rise and were met by the rebels. Allen was numb with a soldier's duty, a brutality disguised by action, simple as the age-long carnal nature that ruled the species of mankind.

Like a blessing, a brief lull surrounded Allen, and he strove to gain his bearings. Just then a movement caught Allen's eye off to his right. A lone soldier struggled to right a flagstaff from beneath a dead body. Something about the soldier had Allen riveted on him. The lanky, skinny form was a dark silhouette before the orange-pink sky that adorned the ridge. The soldier lifted the pole with effort and out from it fluttered the flag. It rose to the sky and the soldier shouted, his tribute voiceless amid the surrounding cacophony.

Bucky! Allen was momentarily rooted to his spot, unmind-ful of the struggle all around him. Then Bucky was running atop the ridge and with force beyond imagination, the youth planted the colors there, proud and auspicious before the enemy.

Allen took off toward the boy as fleet as if he had not run all day, dodging bullets. He came within three yards of Bucky, when the youth went down on his knees. Allen thought he was praying, until he clutched him by the shoulder and saw scarlet seeping from his chest.

Hauling him up over his shoulder, he weaved wildly until he came to a merciful outcropping where three cedar trees met. Hunkering down, he laid Bucky out and pulled back his coat and frayed shirt.

"I did it, Allen. I showed them colors real good. I knowed I could do it."

"Yeah, Bucky, you did it. Listen, don't try to talk. I'm going to get you some help."

"Don't worry, Allen. I don't need no help. I'm 'bout shore Jesus gonna take me home."

Allen ignored him. He pushed on the black hole in Bucky's chest, trying to stanch the blood. Bucky went on, the taut features of his face struggling to smile, "I had to hide most my life, but there weren't no hidin' that flag. I done the company proud. Them colors showed 'em all."

He grimaced. Allen debated which direction to go and reached for Bucky. Bucky lay limp, his smile a faint version of the original. "Aunt Lindy told me God gonna light my candle. He gonna light up the darkness. He is, I know it. It's in the Psalms. You read it, Allen. When you get back, you read about it. For me."

Allen pulled Bucky in his arms. "Hush, now," he hissed. He rose and staggered, but, full of purpose, headed down the ridge toward the scattered regiments. He saw white-covered wagons in the distance, glowing like lilies in the pre-dusk evening. Ambulances, Allen prayed, desperation seizing him. "Just hang on, Bucky. I'm going to get you some help. Bucky?"

The figure in his arms grew light in a strange way. The face was smooth, blissful. A whisper came faint, yet audible in the incredible destruction all around. "Them colors was like a light, just like my candle be, Allen. All lit up, way up there. You read about it. For me. Promise?"

110

Allen huffed, gaining momentum. He carried the slight form right up to the wagons, safe now behind Federal lines. He handed Bucky over to an orderly, like an offering, his gaze frozen on the placid face.

"He's gone, fella."

In the gathering darkness, Allen peered harder. He seized Bucky's collar and pulled him closer. "Bucky? Wake up! I promise, okay? I promise!"

The orderly caught Allen's arm. "Take it easy, man. I said, he's gone."

Distraught, Allen backed away. He shook his head, wanting to clear away the dizzy delirium that threatened to engulf him. He sank slowly into the shadows the trees offered, momentarily confused.

An officer barking orders broke through the hazy web that enveloped Allen. He broke free of it and remembered his duty, suddenly pressing in intensity, as though Bucky needed restitution.

Allen strode from the shelter of the trees, out into the open, toward the battleground. The senselessness of Bucky's death warmed his innards several degrees. Banked embers were fanned, and Allen resolutely started towards the fight. In his mind, there was a great equivalence between "white" and enemy.

Down over the valley, night crept stealthily onward. A smoky, gray column was visible below—rebel reinforcements. The word came borne on the air like the sparks that burned at clumps of dry brush that General Burbridge was calling his men to retreat.

Allen could hear drums rolling off the ridge. His frustration mounted. He clambered beside his comrades, his mind reeling furiously. They had not captured the salt works after this whole momentous day. Retreat meant defeat. The savage cry that rose to his lips poured forth like a death wail in intensity. Then as sudden, the angry war cry was silenced.

Allen stood stock-still and felt a strange sensation. Looking down, he saw crimson spreading across his thigh. It was like a red army that surged across the blue wool of his pants, conquering until it amassed the cloth. Stunned, Allen placed his hand upon the flow. As the realization he had been wounded made imprint on his consciousness, a volley of canister exploded overhead. Then fiery metal rained down, blacking out Allen's knowledge of any world.

Chapter 18

November 1864

The Expulsion

Lucy could not keep the bitterness at bay. Here, in the pre-dawn darkness of November 24th, was another expulsion and Lucy's family was now a part of it. "Cleaning house" was all the explanation given; the women and children left in the camp were being herded like cattle onto the compound and told to go make homes beyond the camp.

Lucy minded the officers who shouted as if the women were deaf. She minded being driven like an animal, with the soldiers holding guns. But mostly she minded the hurt. She had come to feel valuable here, but suddenly was no longer. It felt just like being a slave, used until the white folks got tired of you.

"Mama, I don't understand." Lucy's voice trembled. Mama did not speak. Her eyes were focused on the officer in charge.

When she tore her gaze from him, she whispered, "Now is not the time. Best shore up, Lucy, for what lies ahead."

Mama's dire words caused a river of fear to course through her. Narciss' anxious face was bleached with a paleness that resembled Lucy's.

Ruby, Ruby's daughter, and Naomi, friends since they had come to the camp, joined them as they were forced out. Each carried only a few personal belongings. They were not allowed even the wool blankets on their cots.

Lucy noticed immediately how thin her shawl was against the elements of November. Early this morning, the mercury claimed below freezing and a gusty wind tore at them. Looking over the crowd of women, most possessed worn clothing or shawls hardly competitive to the chill of early winter.

Out of the gates they went, bewildered over this unexpected upheaval. Who would cook and wash for these men? They needed her, these soldiers in blue. Hadn't she done her share of work to make the camp a success?

Where were Rev. Fee and Miss Fair? Why did Captain Hall not stop these men? These thoughts mulled in Lucy's mind as she watched with disbelieving eyes as the soldiers trampled down the shanty houses and tents clustered around the camp's perimeters. The shabbily dressed occupants tore out, clutching a child or blanket. Down went the only structure that housed them. From somewhere a few ox carts came and began loading women and children, to carry them towards Nicholasville, anywhere away from the camp.

The soldiers' refrains grew distant in Lucy's ears. Their shouts only spoke in a diabolical language: *No matter if your husband serves our country, our gratitude is unscrupulous, and you are little to us except a burden.* The honesty of this made her eardrums grow quiet. All the bellow in the world could not touch the numbness there. Lucy felt her heart breaking for herself and these wives being cast aside.

A soldier motioned to Mama, "Get on here!" Mama surveyed the cart, packed precariously with women and children. They would be driven off and dumped at some destination. Then they would have to eke out some livelihood or beg in unfriendly streets. Maybe their former masters would reclaim them or maybe they would be forced to go back on their own.

Once Mama would never have disobeyed a white man. Now Mama shook her head and turned to her girls. She cast mournful glance at the huddled groups, undecided where to go. "We rode into this camp, girls, but we sure aren't going to ride out. We'll walk. Come on." Mama strode purposefully around to the women and encouraged them to remain together. "There's safety in numbers. Let's join together for now."

Lucy stood watching. Mama tenderly wrapped little ones and shushed bawling babies. She spoke soothingly to distraught mothers. Narciss grasped Lucy's arm and propelled her forward, and Lucy let herself be caught up in the role of comforter too. She was a veteran here at the camp, giving her an invisible means to be of service.

As the women trudged on toward Nicholasville, Lucy looked back. Sentries surrounded the perimeters, ready to bar anyone's return. Already the collection of dwellings was reduced to rubble. Lucy felt a surge of hot blood course through her temples, warming the chill within her. She directed her words to Mama. "How can they do this? How can they? After all we've done here. We were a part of that camp!"

Mama looked resolutely ahead. She would not look back. "White men don't need no reason to send you here or there. Always been that way and always will be, until we get to that River Jordan."

Lucy was not satisfied. The answer hurt. Somewhere inside, Lucy's heart felt rent with questions about loyalty and betrayal. Must she surrender the ideals of truth and friendship as false apparitions? They did not seem to exist in her world. Indeed, did they anywhere?

They walked for hours until they came to a lone decrepit barn, set back from the road. Its weathered gray sides buckled at the bottom and two shuttered openings above reflected empty eyes. Inside, deserted clumps of straw lay in heaps. A few deleted cobs of corn littered the floor in an otherwise barren barn.

Mama led them inside and eyed the above rafters with their missing shingles. "Let's start a fire to warm by. Then we'll work on something to eat." Those able searched for firewood.

After they had helped make the little children comfortable, the women began the task of finding food. Narciss and Lucy found a few nuts in the woods surrounding the old barn, but November did not offer much to glean. As they trooped back to the group, Lucy's heart felt deadened; the tender tissue hardened.

She spoke savagely, "Why didn't Rev. Fee stop this? Where was Miss Fair? Do you think they only pretended to be our friends?"

Narciss looked shocked, "Oh, Lucy, don't. You're angry and hurt, is all. There's a reason. There's got to be."

Lucy reflected on her sister's words, but her anger against the camp refused to diminish. More calmly, she asked, "Aren't you, Narciss? Aren't you angry over this?"

"Sure I am. But I've got hope Miss Fair is trying to get us back. It's probably all a big mistake." Lucy's ire temporarily abated.

Once back, the group settled for the rest of the day and night to rest. Their numbers consisted of eleven women and five children. Many of the women were sick or had a sick child. All shivered with cold and took turns around the fire.

Mama clustered beside her daughters. "I'm worried over those sick ones. It's drafty in here, and what will we find to eat?" Lucy had no answer. She listened to the boards wince under the wind's pressure. That sound was broken by intermittent coughs of the ill.

"Tomorrow we'll go try to round up some food. We must pray for guidance, girls."

The night was fitfully long. Two of the children had fevers and three women moaned and retched through the night. They lay on the used straw, sharing blankets and huddling for warmth.

The next morning, three more refugees appeared, one an older man. By noon, five more joined them. All had been turned away from the camp.

Thomas, an older slave, told them about further develop-

116

ments. "They turned everyone away. Tore down all the quarters we had built there. People wandering everywhere. No food and freezing. Seen an old woman just lay down on the road and she never got up again. Little babies can't take the cold, they just dying in their mama's arms."

Mama's sorrowful face reflected everyone's sadness, but she worked at making those in need comfortable. Several left to search for food. Lucy went out and asked at a farmhouse, where a woman kindly gave her some cornbread. It did not go very far divided among so many.

Lucy's walk had left her limbs feeling like wooden attachments. Her stomach hurt from emptiness, and her mood was gloomy as the November day.

Mama improvised to make soup for the sick. Someone had a beat-up kettle and Thomas appeared with a chicken. No one asked where it came from. He brought more news.

"Refugees clear up to Nicholasville, camping out everywhere they can find a place. Most of them pretty sick on account of the weather. They said that General S.S. Fry ordered us out. Wonder how that man gonna sleep at night? But you know there were people starving even back at camp. They didn't share no rations with all us outside those gates. There was some pretty hungry people. Some said they might be eatin' each other."

At the women's horrified looks, he remained nonjudgmental. "People drivin' to do hard things in hard times. We all know about it, don't we? War makin' it more harder all the time."

Unruffled, Mama spoke, "Everything's got to end sometime, good or bad. Best to keep our wits about us." Her look brooked no more rumor talk.

Lucy's time was spent stroking a brow or offering words of encouragement, though she felt little of it herself. When she wasn't doing these things, she sat staring into a fire that warmed only her outer skin. Inside her heart was a hard, cold lump, which memories failed to touch. She crouched and reflected on the course of things. Why had their friends not stopped this horrible predicament? Did not God see their suffering condition?

She felt betrayed.

Her past life seemed distant, when she had felt useful and so certain of her place. She should never have believed the future looked bright. This was a different drumbeat to which she knew no step, allowing bewilderment to seep into her marrow. The only familiar thing was the desperation, which she had once been kin to, now returned and cleaved to her like a long-lost relative.

Startling her from her reverie, a figure burst into the barn. It was Rev. Abisha Schofield. He greeted Mama warmly and said, "I've brought a wagon of supplies. Some foodstuff and clothing. Blankets."

There were several glad cries, and Lucy gasped to see Miss Fair step out from behind the Reverend. Her face was tired but she had a smile for each of them. They had been traveling for the last two days, trying to help all those they could.

"I'm so glad we found you, Angelina." Miss Fair told Mama. "Here. Let's distribute the blankets."

In a few hours, everyone was in better spirits and better equipped for the cold. Rev. Schofield and Miss Fair were going on, to reach other refugees in need.

"We'll be back by, to see how you're faring," Miss Fair promised. She paused, taking Mama, Lucy and Narciss into her confidence. "Rev. Fee was away during the expulsion. He's coming now to see to all this. So was Captain Hall. He was in Lexington and he's outraged over this ordeal. He's asked for General S.S. Fry's resignation. It's all so awful."

After they left, Lucy dwelled on Miss Fair's news. It was an explanation, yet her heart still sought the knowledge of how this could have come about.

The next day, more refugees came to join them. Morale was low. Mama had taken to singing her treasured spirituals and hymns. Lucy and Narciss followed suit although Lucy had to force herself. It helped pass the time and quiet the children. Lucy kept busy gathering dry wood and doing things to entertain the little ones.

Late that afternoon, Rev. Schofield came back. In his arms,

he carried Miss Fair. With shallow breaths, he laid her on a makeshift bed that Mama scrambled to arrange. "She's succumbed to the fever. She's worked so hard these past days." He wrung his hands. "She won't let me take her to the camp, and I fear they wouldn't let her in, as it is."

Mama took in the situation quickly. "We'll care for her here. But ...." She hesitated and looked around helplessly.

Rev. Schofield nodded. "I'll be back with more provisions."

Lucy could not leave Miss Fair's bedside. She stroked her forehead, longing to see those peridot eyes gazing at her. She wanted to will that beautiful smile of Miss Fair's to light up the barn. Instead, Miss Fair lay quiet, two pink spots flushing her thin cheeks. She tossed and murmured fitfully.

"Mama, Mama," Lucy groaned. "Why must she suffer? She's so good and sweet and ...." Lucy's voice trailed off.

"Oh, child," Mama said, her hand on Lucy's bent head. Then she knelt beside her. They watched Miss Fair's laboring breath. "Why is anything the way it is? There's no answers to most of life's questions. We aren't strangers to hard times, Lucy. We've seen plenty and we'll see plenty more. Just got to make the best of things. We're here, in a shelter, and Rev. Schofield has found us. Some of those poor souls are just wanderin' around out there." Mama grew quiet. They sat, side by side, for a long time.

Mama spoke again, "You pray, Lucy, it's part of our duty. Pray for Miss Fair and God's will, not what you be wantin'. You pray for your young man, too. He's going through things we can't even imagine." Mama stood up, and went to care for the sick. Lucy sat, full of Mama's thoughts. Eventually she rested her head on her knees, and directed a weak shadow of petitions heavenward.

For days, Miss Melinda Fair hovered between this world and the next. She grew thin and weak. Her robust, pretty skin turned gray. She no longer would wake even to drink.

Then one evening, her eyes opened. She looked up at the

rafters overhead and sighed. Lucy was dozing beside her pallet when she felt the motion. She sat up hastily, scrambling to come into Miss Fair's view.

Miss Fair saw her. "Lucy." Her voice was weak and croaky with disuse. Lucy spoke rushed words. "Oh, Miss Fair, you're awake! You're going to get better. Rev. Schofield is bringing more food ...." Something in Miss Fair's eyes stopped Lucy.

"Lucy. You are a dear friend. You spoke the truth. Capt. Hall is a good man. I wanted to be his partner, in saving our people. I felt so alive and happy working with him. But that's all it ever was. Always Capt. Hall was honorable. It was me. I wanted his admiration and yes, maybe even his love."

Lucy shook her head. She didn't want Miss Fair to tell her all this. She wanted her to sit up and smile. "No, Miss Fair, please, don't!"

Melinda Fair spoke again, "Real friends tell us the truth. I needed to hear that, Lucy, before I–before I made a fool of myself. I'm sorry, Lucy. Sorry I pulled away from you, such a good, true friend."

Lucy felt tears wetting her cheeks. "No, really, Miss Fair. It's me who's sorry. You've been a wonderful friend to me."

Now Miss Fair's voice was a mere whisper as she struggled to speak, "It looks like my work here is finished. Don't forget me. Remember to be independent and do the right thing. Then you'll never be sorry."

"Oh, no, please don't, Miss Fair. I can't stand it!" Mama gripped Lucy's shoulder and Narciss knelt beside them, tears streaming from her eyes as well.

And then Miss Fair's spirit found release. She smiled a beautiful beam, filled with a glory and wonder Lucy had never before witnessed, as if the barn rafters had become a cathedral filled with an angelic host.

Lucy buried her face in her hands and wept.

Chapter 19

January 1865

Spring Hope

Lucy found herself on her way back to Camp Nelson. Orders had been reversed, and the refugees were now going to find homes there within the gates. Lucy did not know that many people had been brave and courageous in bringing to light the full horror of the expulsion. Word spread by telegraph and the ink quill bore record of the misery. United States Secretary of War, Edwin M. Stanton, took up his pen to stem the suffering, and the injustice was known abroad. In Kentucky, a muted consolation came. Families belonging to a soldier were free as of March 3, 1865.

Rev. Fee also had arrived, directing and encouraging the refugees. They were placed in warm barracks with stoves and adequate food, along with medicine. Often Lucy saw Rev. Fee carrying a glass bottle around, full of dark tonic, dispensing it liberally.

Lucy and her family carried on in their nursing duties. Once again she toted a wooden bucket. From within its confines, she gave fresh water to the sick, held it for those who retched, and cleaned up those sick with dysentery. Every time she stepped out back to throw the slops, she held her breath and wanted to cry, but could find no release. Her heart still smoldered over the treatment they had received and mourned Miss Fair's untimely passing.

The universal wooden bucket, used for work and for nurturing, became a symbol of hopelessness to Lucy–its duty was never done and there appeared no end to it.

More people became sick due to the exposure during the expulsion. They began to die in droves. The 124th Colored Infantry had returned to become the burial detail. Every time a blue uniform came into the barracks, Lucy shuddered. She became so depressed by it, she could not pray. Her half-hearted attempts eventually dwindled. She would think of Allen and the evenings they spent around the fire, and she was certain it had only been a dream.

Lucy heard Rev. Fee tell Mama he hoped to get an order passed for cottages to be built for the people. "All that fetid air and to be packed in those barracks like hardtack, it has to be unhealthy. It will be cheaper to buy more firewood for the cottages than it is for coffins and graves." Capt. Hall saw the wisdom and granted the request. Soon Lucy saw the homey structures going up and, with little delay, the refugees began moving in.

How Lucy longed to step right back into her old routine. She wanted to cook, wash and bake, but now she was considered a refugee, and they would not employ her. All she could do was nurse the ill. She could not even learn anymore since Burritt Fee had been sent away due to the sickness. She grew weary in mind and heart. She rose and followed Mama, performing her duty stoically, in a crazed gray world of sickness.

*　　　　　*　　　　　*

Narciss stood at the door of the cottage and let her eyes adjust to the interior. Then she waited. She watched her sister's movements. They were graceful but mechanical. Lucy served water, dipping the tin cup full, weaving between beds with her offering. No one would guess her mind was tucked away somewhere else. But it was, living far from her task as water bearer in the cottage. Narciss knew. And what she had to tell her sister would likely send her even further into the recessed caves of her mind. She had not caught her sister's eye so she waited in thought. How should she deliver the news she had just heard? Hand it out in little parcels to let Lucy digest it slowly? Or speak it all in a rush of one sentence and be done?

Then abruptly, Lucy looked up. She stared at Narciss in her white shirtwaist and gray skirt. Slowly she came toward her, as if a lifeline pulled her in from a swirling sea. She knew by Narciss' expression her world was about to change and there was no hesitation. Narciss exhaled.

"What?" Lucy demanded with clear eyes.

Narciss answered, faltering, "Lucy, Allen is on the list this time. He's missing in action."

Lucy nodded, repeating to herself Narciss' words mentally. Missing in action. *What did that mean? No one can find him?* Only one reason presented itself. "Take me."

Narciss took her arm. Lucy left her bucket on the nearest table and let her sister guide her. Both girls were silent as they walked together, slipping through throngs of people.

When they arrived, others milled around the headquarters' clapboard building. Nailed to the walls were the lists of casualties and deaths. Lucy pulled one off the boards. She scanned it until her eyes fell on the "R's". *Ross, Allen, MIA, Battle of Saltville, VA.*

She shoved the paper into someone else's groping hands and looked at Narciss. "That's a good sign, Lucy. MIA is better than–." Narciss' voice dropped off.

Lucy nodded. She let her mind fumble for some sense of this newest piece of upheaval. Abruptly, she spoke, "I've got to get back." Narciss watched Lucy turn away.

As Lucy worked each day, she made herself pray for Allen. It was not because she didn't want to. She was just certain God did not care, that He had turned absent ears on her prayers or blind eyes where her life was concerned. She did it because it seemed to her like ol' Cissie's voodoo stuff. If you didn't, you might incur more wrath.

She turned one day down the thoroughfare and past the corrals when she heard the word "massacre". Frozen, she turned slowly to listen to a group of idle soldiers.

"That's what it was! Plain and simple! Any wounded that were left behind were butchered, just killed where they lay. The rebs just can't stand the idea of us fighting them."

"They went into the hospitals and killed them in their beds too. Even the white officers over them."

Lucy hurried up to the soldiers. She clutched the sleeve of one of them. "What battle?"

The men grew quiet. No one answered. But Lucy did not waver. "Tell me."

One spoke reluctantly, "Saltville, Virginia, ma'am."

Lucy swallowed painfully. She was unsure what the possibilities might be. She suddenly thought of Rev. Fee. He would tell her the truth.

Rev. Fee was reclining in his wooden chair behind his desk when Lucy barged in the schoolhouse. Startled, he dropped his feet from the desk, looking rather shame-faced. "Lucy, is the house afire?"

She arrived at his desk, breathless. "Rev. Fee, please tell me the truth. Could Allen Ross be dead? They said they killed the wounded black soldiers on the field at Saltville. Could it be so?"

Rev. Fee pursed his lips. "Well, Lucy, we don't know that anything is so. Yes, I've heard they did harm those left behind, but you don't know if he was left there or already behind the lines. It will do no good to surmise or worry. For now, he is missing, which gives us hope."

Lucy felt desolate. Instead of comfort, she felt as if answers eluded her purposely. The mockery was on someone's part and

Lucy felt largely upon the One in charge. Anger was the easiest emotion to dredge up.

She burst out. "Of course! Hope. What is there left to hope for? If God cared one little bit, He would answer ME! He doesn't care! He isn't listening to me because He doesn't care! I'm not white!"

"Lucy–." Rev. Fee spoke severely, but Lucy whirled and tromped out before he could finish. Chagrined, Rev. Fee sat down heavily. He knew how bleak things looked. What more could he offer for encouragement than the belief of hope? Was it not described as "an anchor of the soul, both sure and steadfast"?

He rubbed a heavy hand across weary eyes. He missed his family and worried over their often frail health. His spirit was troubled for the atrocities that the war had engendered. He nearly wished his work on this earth was done except for that little filigree-toned hope that adorned the brooch of his life.

John G. Fee cradled his head in his arms upon the desk and allowed himself a few moments of weakness to hide his moist face.

Lucy wallowed in indifference. If God did not care, she would not care about Him either. Mama would frequently watch her daughter with concern. She worried over Lucy's withdrawn attitude. The busy schedule they all were apart of was both helpful and disarming. Mama hardly had time to talk to her daughter. All Mama's life she had felt words did little to ease life, but maybe now was the time when words could. Mama felt an idea grow, one she thought on while she moved between the beds of the sick. She would see Rev. Fee about it.

Rev. Fee sought out Lucy when she was at the pump house. He came up quietly, seeing Lucy's mind was far from her task at hand. "Lucy?"

Her gingham shoulders turned and she nodded at him. No smile or greeting. He pressed on. "I've brought you something." He held up a brown volume. "I was thinking about how much you wanted to learn and with Burritt in Cincinnati, well, what if I teach you? We'll be having classes again. Your mother said it was all right. The sick are recovering enough for you to take some time off. How about it?"

Lucy dropped her eyes. A faint stirring within her chest prompted her to meet his eyes. "I could try it. Don't suppose I remember much."

Rev. Fee grinned. "Here. You take this and practice. I'll see you tomorrow afternoon for lessons." He handed her the book. Lucy took it and watched Rev. Fee's gray-clothed back grow smaller, swallowed up by the blue uniforms of passing soldiers. She pondered the book, but did not open it. Could she still learn? She had been able to read Allen's name on the list. Her eyes fell to the bucket of water. The clear liquid reflected back her face—pale even in her reflection. What had Allen seen in her? Had he really asked her to share his name? It seemed a lifetime ago, him treading backward down the thoroughfare calling to her about the picture she made. Then again, here at the pump house, where they had first met.

How Lucy wanted to cry! She felt her tightened breath, the throbbing in her temples, the sharp pricks of pain behind her eyes. But she could not, would not, cry over God's indifference of her life. She would outlast the pain and show Him she was just fine without His care.

She clutched the book under her arm and carried her water to the cottages for Mama. She watched the sun peek out from behind gray clouds. For a moment, she thought of Miss Fair, how her smile had felt like sunshine on a dreary day. Wouldn't she be glad that Lucy was going to learn again? She would be honoring Miss Fair's last words. She would not forget her, ever, and she would be independent, since there was *no one else* she could rely on.

Lucy took the brown volume out from under her pillow. Doubt shadowed her thoughts, but she put on a clean apron and went to the schoolhouse. It was nearly full of women and children. Rev. Fee's eyes lighted on Lucy and he nodded encouragingly.

For the next hour, Lucy chanted and practiced letters aloud with the group. When the lesson ended, she broke out into the cold raw air in relief. She had remembered a lot of what Burritt had taught her, and she was going to learn to read.

That evening, as she stretched on her cot, she thought on the health that her family had during the whole ordeal of the expulsion. Lucy did not credit God with granting them a blessing like Mama and Narciss did. Rather Lucy was sure that being relegated to cleaning up after others so near the brink of death was just some twisted way to squeeze a little more drudgery out of her and force even more unhappiness into her dreary world. She shuddered.

Her thoughts sought that special alcove in her mind where hid precious glimpses of Allen. In these reminiscences she heard his voice and his laughter warmed her. The time she had shared with him had been so fleeting, and she had been so blind.

Carefully, disciplined, she would wrap the memories up like a gift and tuck them away on the shelf of her mind. She lay there, searching the darkness for the sight of the familiar beams above. She reminded herself it was all over. Allen was gone. He would not return for that small kiss she had so stingily withheld. Her heart, nearly suffocated by what might have been, told her she would never love again.

When Lucy had gone to school for a month, she could read and write fluently, and Rev. Fee was quite proud of her. "My dear girl, you've mastered your studies so well, you are ready to move on. Here, maybe this is something more challenging for you." He thrust a slim bound Bible at her.

Lucy did not want to appear rude but the last book she wanted to study in was that one. "I have my primer, Rev. Fee. Thank you anyways." She backed away to leave.

Rev. Fee's gaze pinned her to the floorboards. "Lucy, you aren't fooling me one bit. You're holding a grudge. Now you're not the only one who has done it, but it's time to get things straightened out."

Lucy did not move. A trapped feeling suddenly ensconced her. Rev. Fee continued, "Things have been tough, but there is a right place and a wrong place to lay the blame. I can see you've done yourself admirably, waiting and caring for the sick like you have. Not many young ladies could stomach it. For all appearances, you have dedicated yourself beyond a Christian's annals. But underneath, I sense you are unrestful and the joy is gone."

Lucy could only utter one word, "Joy?"

"Yes." Rev. Fee continued, "You know I'm always up to a sermon, but I'll be brief here. You've lost your joy in life and where most Christians find joy in serving God, you've most certainly regressed. Tell me why?"

Lucy looked at this great man, whose name she had associated with Benefactor and Shepherd. How could she put into words what smote her heart?

"You've lost two dear friends and felt cast aside. But maybe some wrongs have been righted. Maybe not. Yet you have blessings you are discarding because of unrighteous feelings. You must stamp them out now."

Lucy half-turned. In a voice akin to a whisper, she spoke, "When will it be enough, after all I've gone through? You know I acknowledge Him? I know He's in control. It's just a senseless uncaring kind of control."

Rev. Fee prompted, "And if He won't give you what you want, why should you believe?" Lucy was quiet.

"Lucy, Lucy. Don't you know how it hurts God to see all this pain we are inflicting upon each other? All by the ones He created in His image. Man has a choice, Lucy. We can live godly or not. It all has its consequences. But the last one to want our hurt is God. Things happen because of man's choices and at the base of that lies his sinful nature. You can't blame God for that."

"What about Miss Fair's death? Why wouldn't He listen to my prayers? Whatever did she do to deserve death?" Lucy's eyes flashed and her fists were clenched.

Rev. Fee carefully caressed the cover of the black Book in

his hands. "What makes you think death is evil? It can be a very blessed release. Melinda is now beyond pain or evilness. She is in the Lamb's bosom. I think you are thinking of yourself. You miss her but what of her eternal gain? Can you wish her back?"

Lucy looked at the Bible in Rev. Fee's careworn hands. She moistened her lips. "I've never thought of it that way."

"No," Rev. Fee said softly, "We hardly ever do. But remember our ways are not His ways. He is far above us in His infinite wisdom."

Lucy considered Rev. Fee's words. But God was responsible for all things, was He not? She voiced her thought and waited on the reverend's answer.

"Lucy, He knows all things and what will happen before we do. Even the hairs on your head are numbered and He knows. But as for why God places the things in our path that lie there, that belongs to Him. This I do know: It is for our eternal good, even if we don't understand. And I know He loves us. We must just have faith and trust, and the hardships we endure will temper us like fire and make us an acceptable offering in His sight. It's the highest calling of mankind. Do you understand?"

Lucy nodded but she had much to contemplate. Hesitantly, she asked, "He could stop the bad things, couldn't He?"

Rev. Fee smiled, "Yes, He could. But remember the Lord's Prayer? 'Thy will be done, in earth as it is in heaven.' We pray for His perfect will in our lives, not for our own feeble will to prevail."

Lucy reached out and took the Bible from Rev. Fee's hands. She tucked it against her side; a humbled stance adorned her thin shoulders. "I'll practice my reading." It was all she would consent to.

Rev. Fee masked the twinkle in his eye, turning toward his desk. "Good girl, Lucy. I'll see you tomorrow."

Gradually and barely perceptibly, the camp began to change. Families found one another. The sick grew well. The dead in their graves began to be covered with sparse new grass. Spring had come.

Lucy traded her bucket for a frying pan. She got work more to her liking, yet her heart felt like a stone, unable to wake up to the call of the season.

More buildings were under construction: new schools, a mess hall and meeting houses. A rush of people came, some white and some black. New organizations and aid societies brought people of different religions to minister. Schoolteachers came in droves to teach and arm Lucy's people, because the war was ending. Lucy heard how General Lee's army of confederates must surrender soon. They were in a worse way than the slaves: no shoes or ammunition, barely clothed and starving. They existed on sheer desperation, which of itself, would give out shortly. Lucy took in the news the same as she drew breath; one sustained her, the other did not. She could hardly believe life would ever be anything other than war and sickness and death.

*   *   *

Allen's first conscious effort came about by the pull of silence. He opened his eyes, small fissures in a soot-covered face, to drink in the darkened sky overhead. The great silence impersonated the night so that Allen interpreted the quiet and darkness as one great entity. He felt relief.

But then his mind, in its natural course of behavior, pricked his conscious and he started. His eyes flew open and he struggled to rise. A waterfall of pain descended upon his head and surged through his body. He lay back, sorting his myriad of confused thoughts for an answer. What had happened to him?

Slowly the flow of time came back—first the battle, then Bucky's death. A fresh pang of hurt followed that realization. Then the retreat and his leg. Moving his hand, he sought out his thigh. It was tender beneath the blood-encrusted torn fabric. He strove deeper into the recesses of his mind, only to recall explosions and thunderous noise.

Murky depths pulled at him, drawing him back into darkness greater than that of the fallen night. Several times he woke, feeling like he was being hunted by bloodhounds, striving to control his mind and body but to no avail.

The evening chill penetrated through his skin, but mostly he felt on fire, like the burning in that certain evil place. He heard the cries of others, moans that like a wind, skimmed the ground to soak into his being.

Seldom now did states of clarity come to him. During one such time, he felt a presence like an invisible wraith, hovering among the moans and cries of surrounding men. He did not cry out; no amount of suffering on his part would so induce him.

Clearly in view, there up above, lights twinkled. Allen noticed them though the weight of the darkness bore down upon him. Those little lights were stars, like flames atop candles. Even as the Presence roamed, the tiny orbs winked down at him, providing comfort. How Bucky would have smiled. Allen exhaled breath into the frosty night. And then coldly, as if a giant Hand swiped them from the sky, the stars blinked out and disappeared.

*   *   *

Alone in the schoolroom, the scent of fresh wood mingled with whitewash. It created an atmosphere of reverence, yet Lucy's dehydrated emotions were not stirred. Instead she sat quietly. She had asked all the questions she had longed to ask. Rev. Fee's answers had lain still, as if in repose, in the grave of her heart.

Lucy placed the black satin ribbon in her Bible and sighed. She had done her best to read and search, hadn't she? She felt her weakness and she offered herself over to the Lord. She wanted to let go of the anger and feel peace. Where was it? There had been no miracle. Where was her trust and faith hiding? She was afraid they no longer existed inside her empty being.

Rev. Fee entered the schoolhouse. He strode over to Lucy and stood before her, looking into her face. He saw the burdened countenance, the longing buried within her, collected in the mirror of her eyes.

"Lucy," he said huskily. "You're too young to feel such. You're just weary now. We all are. There is a time for everything under the sun. Isn't that what the Book of Ecclesiastes tells us?"

Still Lucy was quiet. She raised her eyes openly to his face. It was a good sign, Rev. Fee concluded. He continued, "You have much pain in your heart, Lucy. You must let go of it, be free of it. Then you will heal.

"The Lord knows all about it. Didn't this evil world kill His only Son? We mustn't be on equal terms with our enemies. It'll make us unrighteous. We must rise above or we will be overcome.

"'Overcome evil with good' we are told." Very gently, he gripped Lucy's wrists with his hands. "This tempest is about weathered. One day you'll look back and see the good it has wrought in your life. You will gather strength from it. And the spiritual things–faith, hope, love–these cannot be killed like the body. They can always be revived."

He stood slowly, looking down on the young girl with sorrow etched on her face. When Lucy looked up, she saw two unshed tears in her benefactor's eyes, brilliant as diamonds. "Remember the promise in Revelation? 'To him who overcometh will I grant to sit with me in my throne, even as I also overcame, and am set down with my Father in his throne.'"

"Spring has come, Lucy, to Camp Nelson. A renewal of life. Go out these doors and look over the green hills. Once more we have seedtime and harvest. And hope. You go out there and see the beauty once more. Let go of the pain. Even an old man like me still looks for God's promises in the small things. They're there, you know." He smiled and in its own way, it rivaled Miss Fair's beam.

Lucy watched that smile grow and saw Rev. Fee's encouraging nod. "See there, Lucy. Your heart is melting, another of God's promises. 'I will never leave thee, nor forsake thee.'"

Lucy felt her lower lip quiver, while her eyes tingled. She put a hand to her face to dam up the raging torrent that resided there. Once she started, the current would rent itself, and Lucy would be powerless to ebb the flow. She had not cried since before the expulsion.

"There, there," Rev. Fee spoke soothingly. He knew the healing power of tears for a distressed soul. They would help wash away the anguish. He moved across the schoolhouse confines, giving privacy to the weeping girl. Looking back, he assured himself the tears were of a healing quality. Then he stepped out to face the rolling hills of the camp. They were indeed green. Sprightly wildflowers adorned them. No truer testimony of life existed on this side of Heaven. Satisfied, Rev. John G. Fee turned and pulled the door shut. He slipped his hands into his pockets and strolled away.

Chapter 20

1865

Recovery

The slave cabin wasn't familiar and yet, Allen knew in a sense that was where he was. Leaning up on his elbows, he took in the surroundings similar to the ones that he had come into the world with. The pain in his head made his thoughts fuzzy in a queer way, but he knew by the worn wallboards and the dirt floor. A rickety table filled the center of the small cabin and there was a fire in the hearth. Allen realized he was on a bed against the wall, facing the doorway. Bright sunlight streamed through, burning his eyes, so he lay back, causing more pain in his head. He winced.

The doorway darkened and Allen lifted his head once more to see. Not until the shadow came close could he make out the figure of an old man. The old man, bent from the waist, peered closely at Allen.

"You awake, huh now, young fella? Good, good. It be time, I sure say. Thought maybe you gonna sleep your life away. Be a shame, I say."

Allen lay transfixed, listening. His tightened muscles relaxed slowly. The old codger seemed harmless. "Where am I?"

The man shuffled slowly around the room, hanging a kettle on a metal hook over the fire. "You be wantin' some tea. It'll taste good to that dry crawl of yours, I 'spect. You laid there for some weeks now. Didn't know if you gonna live or die." He pulled up a wobbly chair beside Allen. "Now let's see. What you ask me, boy?"

Allen wet his dry lips. "Where am I?"

"You be on the Collins' farm. Virginia." He waited on Allen. Allen felt his leg. He wasn't wearing his uniform. He looked down at himself and struggled to rise.

"It'll be alright, boy. You're safe. You wearin' my son's clothes. Hard to come by, but–well, he got some spares from the bodies he be buryin'. Your uniform is washed and waiting. Bessie did it for you while we waited to see if you gonna live."

Allen settled back, a hand rubbing his temple as he tried to ward off the percussion that traveled through his head. "Well, obviously I'm alive. Tell me the damage." He gritted his teeth.

The old man smiled, so that his face resembled a brown wrinkled apple core. Black eyes shone like juicy raisins. His laugh rumbled in his chest but leaked out quiet-like. "You have a bump on the head. It was swollen real bad but it ain't so big now. Lots of blood everywhere. Your leg just sliced up a bit. It was infected, but Bessie cleaned it out and your fever went away. Then you sleep like a baby."

Allen studied his leg. He wore strange trousers but underneath, he could feel it bandaged. He rubbed over his head, tender all along his scalp above his right ear.

The old man hobbled over to the fire and poured some water into a cup, adding a little cloth bag to steep. After a few moments, he squeezed the bag of water and brought the tea to Allen. Gratefully, Allen accepted the chipped cup and drained it. A million questions pressed on his mind, but for the present, he savored the quiet and the safety the old man offered.

Then without quite realizing it, he grew sleepy, leaning back on the bed.

While the old man watched, Allen's hand slipped slowly in restful abandonment from the bedside. The old man shuffled at a gait he wasn't accustomed to, to rescue his precious cup from the floor. "That's the way." He spoke to a sleeping Allen. "Glad you chose life, son. Glad you did indeed."

Allen slept for what seemed a long period of time but when he awakened he found the old man at the table, just sitting. Allen watched, curious about his companion, supposing he was reliving memories, the way old folks do.

"I'm awake, " Allen finally announced, hoping for a drink. The old man startled in his chair.

"So you are. " He tottered up to fetch water for Allen, as if reading Allen's mind. "Here, drink up. Plenty of water down at the spring."

Allen drank greedily, realizing he was hungry too. "Bet you're tired of caring for me?" He wondered if the old man was always here, looking after him.

"No, boy, no. I ain't tired of you. Truth is, Bessie brings my food and some for you too. She's spoon-fed you much as I have, only you don't remember. My boy helps out when he can. He's off the farm some, on account not much work here. Massa loans him out. He done lost most his slaves. War ruined his crop and no money to buy seed and replant. They say the war's gonna end. Won't help Massa out any."

"What about you? War's end going to help you out any?" Allen sat up, cramming the cornhusk pillow behind his back for support.

The old man came slowly to Allen's bedside. He settled his light bones in his chair. "Don't think so. I'm too old for help of any kind. Know what I mean?" A soundless laugh came from the aged body.

Allen studied him. "Seriously, if the war ends, you're free. That's what I've been fighting for." He waited for the old man's reply.

137

"Well, now. I never knew my black brethren were fighting in this here war, 'til my boy brought you here. I'd thought you were helping your massa out, waitin' on him and such while he's fighting. Then here you was in a blue uniform." The old man shook his head.

Allen felt a rise of irritation along with the pressure in his head. He pushed on the aching side before speaking. "I haven't been anyone's slave for a long time. I joined up to fight for our people's freedom. This war is going to end with the Union the victor. Then you'll be free."

The old man peered at Allen from a wrinkled mass of wisdom. His eyes bored into Allen's until he became uncomfortable. Then he spoke, "Guess you know why you joined. Young people always need to prove something or settle some score. But for me, free or not, things won't change. I'll live out all my days right here. Too old to go anywhere else. Why, I'm as free here as I would be anywhere."

Allen raised his eyebrows, "You still owned by a white man? He workin' you?"

"Land sakes, no, boy. I haven't worked for a whole decade of years. My massa ain't so bad. I gave my best years to the Collins family, now I just sit all day, gettin' stiff, still gettin' fed."

Allen was sarcastic, "That sounds like a fair trade."

The old man considered. "Mebbe, mebbe not. But since when things been fair? Don't suppose Adam thought it fair he got booted out of that beautiful garden. All on account of a woman." He laughed another noiseless laugh. " 'Course that I understand. My Nora was a beauty. Had she told me to eat some fruit, I'd of done it. That woman could charm me into anything. You got a gal?"

Allen shrugged. "Maybe, if I make it back to her. If she waits for me."

"Oh, she'll wait. Women got more devotion than us men folk do. That's why they be the mamas." Changing the subject, the old man rose. "Must be Bessie is real busy. I'm gonna totter up there to the kitchen and fetch you some dinner. I know

138

you have to be hungry all that sleepin' you done."

After the old man left, Allen hooked his legs over the side of the bed. He tested his legs by trying to stand. They bore his weight and his injured leg had only a faint remnant of soreness. But his head swam as he grasped the wall for support. He would be going nowhere, least of all hunting down a privy on a strange place. He sat down heavily, noticing the bedpan and chamber pot tucked under the cot-like bed.

Allen felt a scalding to realize he had stole the old codger's only bed. The old man had been caring for him, even emptying the bedpan. Why, he didn't even know the old man's name! He was going to remedy that when the old fella came back, along with all the other questions he longed to ask. No more philosophizing.

But when the soup arrived, its smell stole away Allen's curiosity, and he was content to grip the bowl, smiling his thanks at the old man. The questions would wait.

Later, Allen opened his eyes to see a woman in the room, along with the old man. She turned at Allen's movements and came closer. Her frame was large and she had ample meat on her bones. Grey hairs fringed loosely around a yellow turban, which had been home-dyed. She knelt with surprising nimbleness beside Allen, despite her size or age.

"You awake? Good. I brung you supper just now and told Aaron if you don't ever wake up and see ol' Bessie, you be supposin' I'm nothing but a ghost."

Allen returned Bessie's smile. She helped make him comfortable and gave him a bowl of stew.

"Ghosts can't cook this good," he told her.

Bessie laughed. "You be a soldier boy, why, anything would taste good to you!" She stood and shooed the old man to his chair at the table and made sure he ate too. "I got time away from the kitchen. Massa went to his daughters for the evening. I fed the house-folks, then decided to come on down here and see you for myself. You healin' jus' fine, aren't you?"

Allen nodded, wincing a little. "Seems so. Just can't move my head much. Feels like a bunch of loose rocks banging around in there."

Bessie eyed him seriously. "I wonder if that ain't what knocked you out. You were covered in blood, probably not all your own. Dirtiest face I ever seen too. Being a soldier ain't all glory, is it?"

"No ma'am," Allen spoke quietly. "Not much of that."

"You know what happened to you?" Bessie questioned gently.

Allen thought hard. "I remember my leg getting hit, looking at the blood, then–. Well, something exploded, some noise, but that's all I know."

Bessie made a clucking sound in sympathy. She refilled his bowl and checked on the old man to be sure he was eating. She looked fondly at him as she told Allen, "Not much of an appetite. Got to make sure he don't waste away."

The old man gave a mock growl, "Womenfolk! I don't need much, seeing I don't work no more. There was a day I'd have eaten a whole hog I was so hungry, but those days aren't no more."

Bessie humored him. "There's only seven of us left here on the farm. I still be needin' you." She turned to Allen. "You know I'm Bessie and that is Aaron. You'll meet Aaron's son soon, the one who found you. Probably won't see no others. Massa don't know you here, he's got no call to come down to this cabin. We'll keep it quiet, so you're safe, 'til you ready to move on."

Several of Allen's questions had been answered and he felt relief flood his being. Bessie noticed. She spoke, "We been caring for you and we'll keep on, all you need."

"Thanks for everything you've done for me, " Allen said, uncomfortable when he thought of Bessie tending to him. She gave a little rippling laugh.

"No sense turning red, boy. I've cared for five sons. Always was patchin' 'em up, it seemed. Now, tell us your name and whereabouts you from?"

Allen spoke hesitantly. "Allen Ross. I'm with the 6th U.S. Colored Cavalry."

Bessie's eyes met Aaron's. She was direct. "Allen, anything else you care to share? We saved your life. We're not the enemy."

Allen flushed under her rebuke. "I grew up in Kentucky, in Madison County on the Ross farm. There were only twenty of us there, but the master had itchy hands. He sold and traded us around all the time. When Camp Nelson was being built, he took me there to work out. I was glad to get away from the man. Later they said he lost his life in a poker game, so I quit fearing he would come back for me. Then I joined up."

Bessie asked, "You ain't got no family worryin' over you?"

"No," Allen said. "No one left to care."

Bessie collected the dishes and readied to leave. "You just keep restin'. No one bother you here."

Allen motioned to Aaron and the bed he rested on. "I don't feel right taking your bed, Aaron. Maybe I could move to the floor now."

Aaron shook his head. "Another week won't hurt these old bones. Bessie brought me a tick from the house, and I got my blanket. Fire is nice and warm to lie by. You just stay put."

At Allen's doubtful look, Bessie placed an arm around Aaron's wobbly shoulders. "He do anything for you. That's just Aaron's way. It'll be all right. Your head needs more mending. See you tomorrow morning."

After she left, Allen felt like talking. "Tell me about you and this place." He was looking out at the farm beyond the cabin.

Aaron pulled his chair up. "Well, this farm been here since the War of Independence. Given to Samuel Collins from General Washington himself. Now his grandson owns the land. Massa Collins lost most his slaves at the start of the war, jus' seven of us left here. Poor as church mice now, Massa Collins is. Only had daughters, the missus died a few years back, 'fore the war begun. The girls all married, and Massa old and lonely now. He let me live my days out here. He got Bessie and Andrew up at the house, and George and my son, Roy, to mess

141

around on the land. He loan them out too, but not too far. They needed men for buryin' the poor fellas from that battle around Saltville, so Massa let Andrew and my Roy go help. Men on both sides, lying all around. That's how Roy got some more clothing. Fellas didn't need it no more. Sad business, whole thing." Aaron hung his frosted head and sighed. Then his head came up and he pointed to a blanket in the corner.

"See that blanket over there. Well, thinking on the things Roy found where the fighting was, good blankets even, I have to tell you about this."

He hobbled over to a faded woven blanket of Indian design that he pulled over for Allen to inspect.

"You got this on the battlefield?" Allen asked, incredulous.

"No, no." Aaron smiled. "Just made me think of it. There's a story to this blanket. You got time to hear it?"

Allen smiled back. "I'm not going anywhere."

Aaron cradled it across his lap and studied it with reverence. Allen listened intently. "This blanket is from the Cherokees. My Nora brought it up from the Carolinas, way back when, maybe fifty years ago. She was a slave down there and had a cruel massa. One day she just up and left. Walked for miles 'til she came to the Cherokee lands. She stayed there awhile and when she left them, one of the old wise women gave Nora this blanket. Said she put the good magic in it when she wove it. Nora never had a speck of trouble all the way up here to Virginny. And her ol' massa never found her."

Allen reached out and touched the tight-woven piece. "You think it's got magic in it?"

"Naw. " Aaron shook his head. "But see, when you believe something, you can do 'bout anything. You just plow on ahead, sure-footed and determined, 'specially when you're young. My Nora easy could have crept around, scared-like, and she would of likely been captured. But she strode on out of the Deep South and made it safe."

"Where was she heading? Surely farther north than Virginia?" Allen questioned.

Aaron nodded. "Yes, she was. But she stopped for a drink

at Massa Collin's well and there I was. I got her that drink and that was it for me, let me tell you. Same as if she put a bridle on me. Oh, that gal was a beauty!"

"'Course she was going to move on, but Massa Collins seen her and asked who she was. Well, she told him the truth. My Nora never did lie for no reason! She told him she left a mean ol' massa, and she weren't lookin' for a new one. Massa Collins laughed real hard and told her if she had a mind to, she could stay on and he would give her a cabin and food.

"And that's the way it was. She stayed and cared for the critters. She had a way with 'em, she did. Massa Collins never owned her, Nora said. She felt free. She loved the hills and animals around here, and then, well, she loved me. I was the luckiest man alive and still am. Nora taught me we can still feel free by lovin' the folks around us and our home. I never had no desire to go anyplace else after that.

"See boy, you got the love of one good woman, you got untold riches. You remember that."

Allen nodded, and then asked, "What happened to your Nora?"

"Oh, those critters she loved so much!" The old man squeezed his eyes shut briefly. "She was down at the crick, doing the washin'. Snake bit her. She came up and finished laying the clothes out to dry on the bushes, then called me to come. I was shoeing Massa's mules, but left off and came quick. She was lying down on the bed and told me what happened. 'Guess it be my time, the Lord is calling,' she told me. Then she was gone. I should have wrapped her in her blanket to bury her, but it was all I had of her. And this thing," he continued, hugging the wool blanket to himself, "has kept me warm for twenty or nigh years. Not as good as Nora, 'course, but all right I'd say."

Allen was quiet. Aaron tucked his blanket away in the corner. "You go on and sleep a little, boy. I'll feed the fire."

Allen settled back, thinking of Lucy. Would she be waiting, eager to see him with a welcoming smile, when he returned?

He sought his dreams for an answer.

Chapter 21

Spring 1865

After a few days, Allen decided it was time to try getting around. He felt like Aaron, hobbling toward the door. From there, he had a fair sight of the farm. A red brick house stood on a hill some distance away with a dirt footpath bending towards it. All around were swelling, graceful curves in the land. It was pretty, although not yet touched by spring's hand.

Allen was startled when a black man came into view and sauntered towards him. He backed off the threshold, looking at the approaching stranger's broad face.

"Roy?" he questioned.

The face grinned back at him. "The one and same. You're still in the land of the living, huh?"

Allen gave a laugh, "Come in and tell me how I made it to today." He moved to the table and rested on the corner of it while Roy took the chair. Allen avoided looking at the other man's clothes since he knew how they came to be under

Roy's ownership.

"Where's Pap?" Roy asked, looking around the cabin.

"He's up at the house with Bessie, getting supper. This is the first I've been up. Your old man takes good care of me."

Roy's face held tints of pride. "Folks all around know about Pap. He's always done good by everyone. 'Specially Massa Collins."

Allen agreed. "Told your pappy he was going to be free soon. War's got to end, then he won't belong to no massa. He don't seem to care he's a slave."

Roy shook his head. "Pap's old. He's set, there's no changin' his thinking. Like trying to wring water out of a brick. Old folks just like that." His attention was drawn to Allen's leg. "You're healing up fine it looks like."

Allen said, "My leg's fine but my head is still woozy. I've got to gain my strength back and find my regiment again."

"Not sure how easy that's going to be. But you got time. Leastways it'll keep you from getting shot at. Massa Collins near blind, so you're safe here unless his daughters come to visit. But they don't come down here anyway."

"So tell me how you saved my life." Allen could wait no longer to know.

"Massa Collins said some army people needin' help buryin' the dead. George and I got there and the white soldiers were pointin' out the dead they shot. They were boasting how they went along, shooting any wounded blacks that moaned or moved. Made us near sick!

"They had us to bury our own. We dug a big hole and put all the bodies in together. They had to do the same for the white soldiers on account the ground was too hard to do otherwise. We probably dug twenty pits. Sure is bad work." Roy shook his head.

"Well, I was rolling bodies on a board and rolled you over and you groaned. Scared me, I'll tell you. George looked like you was a ghost. That work gives you the willies anyhow.

"When I heard you again, I knew those white soldiers would stick you through, so George and I put you behind our hill of dirt and waited it out. When they went to eat their din-ner, we carried you to the woods without them seeing us. Then that evening we carried you here. Looked like you was gonna die, but that Bessie could make a dead duck fly if she want to. My mama that way too, taught Bessie all she knows." He paused and watched Allen.

Allen's jaw had tightened, and he realized his muscles were taut. "That's not soldiering in a war, that's plain murder."

Roy shrugged. "Pap says war is murder. He says it's an excuse to force your feelin's on others by killing them off, trying to make yourself right."

Allen's mouth quirked and his eyebrows shot up. "Your Pap thinks the Union is forcing their opinion on the South? He sure is misguided! Where did he get that garbage? Collins?"

Roy held up his hands. "Pap thinks live and let live. He's more of the old peaceful type."

"Well, he's had it good here, apparently. Lots of our peo-ple are suffering at the hands of white men, have been for hun-dreds of years. They need freed. That's why I'm fighting."

Roy listened, then stood. He smiled at Allen. "You're doing a good thing. Pap has his ideas, all right. Hey, you need anything, let me know. I'm going to be around a few days. Massa Collins has me oiling harness and greasing the buggy for spring. Be here before we know it. Virginny sure is beautiful in the spring."

After Roy left, Aaron came back with supper. Allen felt a little peeved with the old man. He ate quietly, and Aaron let him be. Allen stretched out on the bed of cornhusks, listening to the old man shuffle around in the darkened cabin, near the fire.

Guilty feelings surfaced, but Allen batted them away. What kind of thinking did Aaron possess? No one could be happy as a slave! Must be because Aaron was old and didn't care no more. But didn't he care about his son? What future was there for him as a slave? Allen wondered where they would all be if they all felt like Aaron. Even Roy was lukewarm about the subject of freedom. What was their problem? Could they really have it so good here, or were they just really dumb? Allen fell

147

into a troubled sleep.

The next morning, Allen came up behind the old man who was staring out the doorway at the world beyond. He felt like making amends although he had not verbally spoken ill to Aaron. A soft south breeze blew in, which felt like spring arriving. Birds twittered joyfully in a stand of pines not far from the cabin.

Aaron's eyes followed them. "Hear them birds. The birds is the most peaceful and loveliest of all God's creatures. Nora loved 'em. If only people could be as happy."

Allen quickly interjected, "People aren't free like those birds are."

Aaron spoke absently, "No, but our spirit's free. No man can own the soul. That belongs to God."

"Be alright if we were in Heaven. Matters little when we're down here on this earth," Allen spoke behind Aaron's shoulder. The old man turned slowly. His wrinkled face and wizened frame suddenly seemed to grow before Allen. His voice came out strongly from his person. "Allen, you believe that, you got little hope. Don't fall into that trap. Can't always shoulder your way through life. Sometimes got to just be here, occupying, you know. Then it matters who your soul belongs to. Then it matters if you be greater than your circumstances."

Allen said nothing. He had the distinct feeling Aaron knew what he was talking about. He assented by returning to his bed and ignoring the old man.

Like the songbirds, Allen began to "stretch his wings" daily. As he moved around more, he felt himself gaining strength. One day, when Master Collins left with George, Allen trudged up to the summer kitchen where Bessie worked.

"So this is where you create those wonderful meals you're fattening me up with," Allen teased.

"Sure enough. This is my domain. I'm queen here!" Bessie returned with a smile.

"Don't tell me you're like Aaron, happy as hops to be living here, being a slave." Allen couldn't keep the scorn out of his voice.

Bessie stirred a pot of meat bones. She threw in a pinch of herbs without answering. After a moment, she turned. She adjusted her turban, this time a pale faded pink. "I'm not sure I know what you mean, Allen."

Allen exploded, "Roy was telling me about how Aaron feels the war is wrong and how we should be happy where we are–."

Bessie held up her hand to silence Allen. Allen fell quiet, out of respect. She turned to the potatoes that were baking in the coals. After shoving them around in the ashes, she spoke. "I'm fifty-two summers old. Not as old as Aaron, but as I grow older, I understand more what the old folks is saying. So will you, Allen." She turned towards him and spoke, "There's a lot we can say about our spirit. You be happy or you don't. Aaron made the most of his life here. It's what he could do. No sense focusing on what he couldn't do, now was there?"

Allen said nothing. Bessie moved around the kitchen, preparing cornmeal dumplings and stirring up the broth.

"Now you, well, mercy all around! You can do things, Allen. You sure can. If I was twenty-something and a man, you'd see me out doing things."

She shoved a crate at him to sit down on. "I'm just happy I had a good man and six little babies. All of them lived but one, and I still get to see them at times. Even their little ones is nearby. Massa Collins never beat me or starved me. My life's been good."

Allen interjected, "Maybe easy, but not good."

"You are wrong there. Not easy, life ain't never easy. Hard things comin' along all the time, but there be the good if we look for it. We all do the best we can and be thankful. That brings as much joy as we gonna get here."

Allen spoke, "But if you get freed, Bessie, things are going to be good and *easier*. You'll see. Maybe your family can be together."

"That sure sounds good, Allen. Maybe things get better, maybe not. Best not to look too far ahead. Tomorrow always changing, Allen." Bessie removed the meat bones to a platter and bent over the fire to drop the yellow dumpling batter into the broth.

Allen watched, comforted by Bessie's actions since her words left a dark cloud. "Tell me about yourself."

Bessie glanced up sharply, her eyes drinking in Allen's interested face. She continued with her job as she spoke. "I'm from New O'leans. Busy place. My! Virginia's like one of those slow lazy turtles down in the bayous compared to New O'leans."

Allen interrupted, "You have a mean master there?"

Bessie chose her words carefully. "Yes, Allen, I had lots of masters." She paused, working to scrape the wooden bowl.

When she resumed, she smiled weakly at Allen. "But they didn't master me. I survived them, and somehow mercy came my way. I got traded to a white lady. She brought me up by steamboat, up the Mississippi, to Tennessee, 'til I ended up in Virginia. Sold on the auction block, and later given to Missus Collins by her pappy. I came here when she married Massa Collins. My life ain't been all sunshine, but it could have had a lot more clouds, I know that."

Allen didn't know what to say. She had been vague, yet he was disturbed by her sad features while she spoke. There had been great sorrow for Bessie.

"It wasn't an easy life at all. I was only fourteen when–. Well, you got a future ahead of you, Allen. Just remember to take all the good you can out of each day. Be thankful to the Lord."

Bessie then channeled her talk from the present to the future. "You know, we got so much in us black folks. If we all go free, think what good things gonna go around."

"Tell me," Allen prompted.

"Well, all us from places like Africa and Haiti and New O'leans. Places like Florida and Texas–all over the south. Right now, we full of sorrow and our spirits groan. But you know the music that comes from stretching souls? And the joy we have laid up–just waiting to be poured out and flood this country?

150

White people will learn we interestin' folks, not just beasts. Be almost like a new world."

Allen thought about Bessie's words. They held a lot of truth, made a beautiful picture, but he was doubtful. Really, he hardly cared what white men thought. He remembered the days at Camp Nelson when he had wanted to prove how competent he was. The white men there were too self-centered to notice.

He just wanted to make his own place in the world and choose his work on his own time. Just like white men did. He didn't want to worry about ever being sold or his future family being sold away. He wanted all the word promised—freedom.

Bessie's skirts swayed as she moved around the hearth. She hummed as she worked and Allen watched. It brought to mind the days he had watched his own mama moving around, waiting on massa's children and lovingly fetching Allen some stolen morsel from the kitchen. Feelings stirred about more than just his childhood; he thought of Lucy. Would she be his future? Would they build a life together? These thoughts brought raw joy, for the first time in a while he was excited and hopeful.

Then Allen saw the shining revelation Bessie and Aaron spoke of. His pleasant thoughts were neither here nor there. They were miniscule threads of a wonderfully colored ribbon pulled from a rainbow. Suddenly, whether events actually transpired as he had envisioned was not the important thing—what mattered was the joy he felt at that moment. A tingling thread imagined from the glorious ribbon of life, but nevertheless it was very real.

Allen stood shakily and smiled at Bessie. "Bessie." He gripped her arms and looked straight into her eyes. "You don't know all the good you've done me. Or Aaron either. But you've done a lot more for me than just heal up my body. I can never repay you for it."

Bessie's face held a tender look, which broke into a gentle smile. She touched Allen's cheek softly. "You can repay me with respect. Respect for the old folks and respect for other men, both black and white. We got the same soul underneath."

151

She gazed at Allen's face as though seeing a beloved son. "And Allen, you have respect for the life God gave each and every creature. You do that, and you will have repaid me tenfold."

That evening Allen told Aaron he was ready to trade beds. "I'm healed up well enough it's my turn on the floor. You take your bed back."

Aaron fussed but traded blankets with Allen. He put his Indian blanket on his bed and settled under the cover. "Feels good each night to rest these old bones."

Allen agreed, "I'm getting stronger each day, but I'm always glad for nightfall." Allen looked around the cabin in the dusky light. "Know what, Aaron? I was born in a cabin like this, 'cept we never had a table or bed above the ground. We slept on the dirt floor. Then I went to Camp Nelson and had a bunk in the barracks. I was living pretty high on the hog. After I joined the 6th C.C., there I was, back to sleeping on the ground, tenting or worse. Now here I am, back before a fire on a dirt floor. What a journey!"

Aaron's body shook the bed frame with his noiseless laugh. "You know, boy, goes to be that we all come back to the place we started from. Seems we never go far from our own beginning. Ain't so bad, is it?"

Allen watched the red embers glow, casting warmth on the stones surrounding the hearth. "No, Aaron, it's not so bad. I've enjoyed being here with you and Bessie and meeting Roy."

"That so?"

"Yes. It's shown me we can look at things a little differently, but we're nearly all the same inside. We're all wanting basically the same thing, just lots of different ways to achieve it. Right?"

Aaron answered across the darkness. "If you mean you is you and me is me and God gives us good things, then you is right, Allen."

"Good night, Aaron," Allen responded, trying to keep the amusement out of his voice.

"'Night, Allen." In seconds, the old form snored peacefully.

152

Saying goodbye to his new friends proved difficult. Allen had expressed his gratitude, but "goodbye" seemed stuck in his throat. Roy had provided him with a knife and some matches. Aaron gave him the extra blanket he owned. He stuffed his uniform in an old meal bag and readied to go.

He awkwardly hugged the old man and shook Roy's hand. Bessie came down from the kitchen with victuals wrapped in a linen towel. "God go with you, Allen. We're hoping you make it back safely to your army. Here's this." She pressed a New Testament into Allen's hand. "Massa got three or four of these, and he can't hardly see no more. He won't begrudge the use of it. You remember us, Allen, even if our paths never cross again, 'cause we're never gonna forget you."

That evening, Allen sat by a small fire, alone in the woods. He reviewed his time spent with the people of Collins' farm. His head had cleared and no longer bothered him. His leg was left with a scar of new tissue, which stretched around his thigh. The care he had received at their hands was beyond any kindness Allen had ever known.

For the first time, Allen made a point to pray. He looked around the woods where tall dark trees were imposing shadows. Night sounds filled the air, their echoes flitting like bats, swooping toward his ears. Camping out alone suddenly seemed to loom as an intimidating endeavor.

Allen rigidly controlled his thoughts, directing them towards practical matters. He had a journey ahead of him, and he needed to avoid any Confederate soldiers. He hoped they were all together, concentrated in one main body under Lee. He didn't relish meeting up with any stray band of skirmishers. Since he wore ordinary clothing, he might be able to pass off as a slave, unless they found his uniform.

His thoughts pressed on, even after the fire had died, and he had wrapped himself in his blanket against the night chill. Would he find his regiment? And if he did, could he serve with the same earnestness as before? His goal was the same, but somewhere along the way, a mellow understanding had crept in. The goal remained steadfast, the desire as intense, but he felt differently about the means to secure it. He didn't relish the prospect of fighting anymore.

Allen journeyed westward each day, along the same path the army had taken to Saltville. He met up with a donkey in a back pasture and a few ducks along a riverbank but no enemy. His victuals gave out, and he contented himself with new greens for a few days. One evening, he settled under a tree to discover a pair of grouse roosting overhead. As stealthily as he could, he stole upon them and captured one. After his scant meals, he relished the bird and filled his stomach.

One afternoon, he arrived at a farm, where he looked around cautiously. He spied some black folks at the barn. Fortifying himself, he walked near and called out. The men turned at his voice.

"Howdy," they greeted him.

Allen said, "I'm on my way to Camp Nelson in Jessamine County. Am I getting close?"

"Sure are. Probably only a day or so walk from here. Whereabouts you from?" the older of the two men questioned.

"I'm with the U.S. Cavalry. I was wounded at Saltville. Now I'm trying to find my regiment or make it to Camp Nelson first," Allen replied.

The younger man grinned. "You been traveling long?"

Allen's brow furrowed. "Probably eight days. Why?"

"Well, you ain't got no need for your regiment. The war's over!"

Allen's face instantly registered surprise. He felt his heart drop to his kneecaps.

"We're not funnin' you, son. Sure is over. Lee surrendered two days ago, at a place called Appomattox. It's all over with! We're all free!" The two men whooped and clapped Allen on the back. Suddenly Allen was unable to find his voice. He let them draw him to their quarters, where he was persuaded to stay the night. After a warm meal, the news began to vibrate through his being. The war was actually over! Allen felt such relief, it fairly leaked from his pores.

No more fighting. Instead of cannons and artillery, freedom

now reverberated through the South. He had helped, in a small part, to enable the Stars and Stripes to unfurl once more unhindered across a whole nation. And now Allen could claim the promise that awaited him.

Allen angled northward now to Jessamine County. One more night out, and he would arrive at Camp Nelson's gates. For the last night, a brilliant host of stars adorned the canopy overhead. Allen lay back and studied the expanse.

The lights suddenly drew his thoughts to Bucky. "Just like my candle be, all lit up," is what he had said. Instantly, Allen jolted upward. He had made a promise to Bucky, and he had almost forgotten! "It's in the Psalms. You read it, Allen. When you get back, you read about it. For me. Promise?"

Allen hastily pulled his New Testament out of his meal bag. By the firelight, he started reading through the Psalms and then–there it was.

Bucky's treasured verse was the twenty-eighth of the eighteenth Psalm. Allen's finger traced the words. "For thou wilt light my candle; the Lord my God will enlighten my darkness." Allen read on, "For by thee I have run through a troop; and by my God I leaped over a wall."

Allen reread the verses and pondered. Indeed, he had been enlightened. The fear he had held that hatred would force him to kill for vengeance and that he would be no better than his old master had not materialized. He saw that he was not cruel, nor did he enjoy the fight, even when his anger had mounted the greatest.

There was nothing now to fear. He had run through a troop literally and by mysterious ways, he felt he had leaped over a wall. Not only in safety, but the wall of uncertainty had been breached. He was a normal man, but there was no vindictiveness in his heart. God would right the wrongs in His majestic way, in His own time. Allen had come to terms with himself. Tomorrow he would don his uniform and walk into Camp Nelson. The light of his candle, like Bucky's, had not gone out.

Chapter 22

Spring 1865

The Right Way

Lucy and Narciss worked in companionable silence for a while. It was not often they got to work together. This was a special occasion. The girls were baking a cake for Sergeant Ribford's birthday.

Lucy sprinkled a handful of nuts into the batter that Narciss stirred. "Remember gathering these nuts?"

Narciss looked thoughtful. "Yes. Mama sent us to those walnut trees behind the White House. After that job, we had to spread them all out to dry. Remember how Cook Sammy kept kicking them all over the kitchen?" Both girls laughed at the image of a sputtering Sam when he had slipped on the nuts. "Then we had to sit and pick out all the meats with a hairpin for hours!"

They sobered. Those days seemed long ago, when they were girls. In a short amount of time, they had witnessed things that "grew them up" a lot, the way grain ripened in its season. They had not even had a stifling childhood–they had lived through more than many folks had in a lifetime. Their minds subsequently stole to their escape and establishing a home at Camp Nelson, where they had learned to read and write. During the expulsion, the girls had nursed the sick and watched little children close their eyes a final time. Both had lost a dear friend and encourager, and Lucy had lost a love. They had lived through a war and mourned with a nation over the loss of a president.

And it had been no small battle fighting a whole spectrum of emotions spurred by these events. Just like rain and sunshine made the plants grow, life had prompted Lucy and Narciss until they had matured into womanhood.

Their eyes met and they shared a smile and a bond transcending even their blood ties. Lucy's mind returned to her job, and she threw a few more walnuts into the bowl. "Narciss, we're a lot like these walnuts. We started out in green shells, just like slavery, covering us all up. Then the drying process brought about our freedom. The hard shell is our mortal frame, solid enough to withstand all that's been put upon us. And inside, the nut, like our souls, the real treasure." Lucy silently mused on. She looked up to find Narciss staring at her. "What? You don't like that?"

Narciss frowned. "I like the cocoon-butterfly thing better."

Lucy laughed. "You just don't like being compared to a nut!" They worked on until the cake was in the oven, and the kitchen cleaned up.

"There," Narciss said cheerfully. "Now Sergeant Ribford can turn fifty-two. And you can go on and write your poetry down."

"Oh," Lucy returned, "I'm no poet. But maybe, someday down the line, there will be one in the family. We'll have to wait and see what the Lord has planned."

Lucy turned her gaze from the rolling hills. It seemed impossible to believe the war was over, and the nation's leader, the Emancipator, was dead. The army had been coming to

Camp Nelson for days and was being mustered out of service. The camp was to be dismantled, torn apart board for board. The lumber would be gulped up by the county's farmers, who were trying to recoup their losses. Lucy wondered what would be left of it? Would any passerby realize what a place Camp Nelson had been? What it had meant to her?

But it had served its purpose. Just like Rev. Fee said about people. Everyone had a purpose and until it had been fulfilled, they did not leave this earth. This led Lucy's thoughts to the future. What would her purpose be?

Soon Mama had said they would decide where they were going and what they would do for a living. Rev. Fee had bought ground adjoining the camp, to make homes for the refugees. Many were settling down here. Cook Sammy was going to Kansas, where several were migrating for a new life. Lucy's future may once have been decided, if Allen had come back. But she had accepted this change. She could simply live one day at a time and let the future take care of itself.

Lucy, along with a girl near her age, had been readying the White House, the officers' quarters, for their departure. They had cleaned away several months of winter dirt. The spring-cleaning consisted of washing walls and floors and mantels. They had filled lamps and washed globes. The fireplaces were cleaned out and bed ticks washed and re-stuffed. It was four days of work and for the last time Lucy shook out her dust rag over the balcony and set her bucket aside. She swallowed the bittersweet lump in her throat over the hum of activity below her. Then she turned back through the rooms, surveying her labors with satisfaction as she left the upstairs. Everything looked and smelled sweet and fresh. She supposed in time, as the camp was torn apart, it would revert back to its original owners, the Perry family. How outraged they must have been back in '63 to be told by the U.S. government that their ground–all 4,000 acres of it–was being confiscated as government property, and they must leave their beautiful home.

At the top of the landing, Lucy paused. She admired the

yellow poplar floorboards below, radiating their rich tones in the sunbeams. They had not been excessively harmed by the three years of boot tracks.

She caressed the walnut railing of the beautiful free standing staircase that spilled out before her to the entryway. It had been oiled until its dark hue glowed and was satiny smooth. Such a staircase evoked images for even a poor girl like herself.

In her mind's eye, Lucy saw herself adorned in a rich gown, much like one that Fanny Perry might have worn before the war. It would shimmer and rustle and be of a breathtaking emerald green. Lucy had never owned a green dress. Her imagined dress would be of fine silk. She let her mind wander...

    *   *   *

Allen huffed a final time before coming to a halt. He had traveled the Lexington-Danville Turnpike during the last leg of his journey and had arrived at the camp's gates sweaty and sapped out. Each step had brought dregs of fear and uncertainty into his mind and heart. What if Lucy wasn't here anymore? He had been delayed several days by stopping to help out a widow and an old man along his route.

The scene before his eyes caused dismay. Crews of workers, even army men, were dismantling buildings. Piles of used lumber lay stacked. Wagons, loaded with boards, were coming and going. It was a reversal of the sight that had greeted him when he had arrived in camp nearly three years ago.

And then there was an U.S. flag, accompanied by a black one, flying at half-mast. Disturbed, Allen headed to the quartermaster's headquarters, hoping Captain Hall was still in charge.

"Is Captain Hall here?" Allen asked an assistant clerk.

The clerk nodded but jerked a thumb backwards over his shoulder. "The quartermaster is up to his elbows in paperwork. He won't be out before dinnertime, and he asked not to be disturbed."

Allen said, "I'll wait." He went over to a wooden chair and

160

settled in, gathering his thoughts. He watched the officers and soldiers who trooped in for the next hour and a half. Finally the door to the closed room opened. Captain Hall emerged, struggling into his army coat. He looked ruffled and burdened, his shirt collar unbuttoned.

Allen leaped to his feet and approached the quartermaster. "Captain Hall? I'm Allen Ross. Do you remember me?"

Captain Hall puzzled a moment, and then recognition dawned in his eyes. "Yes, Allen Ross. I remember now. What can I do for you?"

Allen briefly recounted his last months and finished, "Has my regiment made it back?"

"The 6th U.S.C.C. came back two weeks ago and was mustered out. I'll get someone to fill out the necessary paperwork for you. As you saw, things are hectic around here. Who would think it would be busier now than wartime?" Captain Hall congratulated Allen on the 6th Cavalry's accomplishments and the Union's victory.

Allen hesitated, as they were ready to part. "Captain Hall, would you know if Lucy and her family are still here?"

Captain Hall's eyes twinkled, "Are there more congratulations in order?"

Allen smiled weakly. "That remains to be seen, sir."

"Well, there is a certain young lady by that name still here. In fact, she's probably cleaning over at the White House, if she's the same one." Captain Hall was amused by Allen's flushed face.

"She's probably the same one, sir."

"Then good luck to you, Private Ross. Good day."

Allen left the headquarters and wandered outside. He once again noticed the flags and remembered he had forgotten to ask Captain Hall about it. He saw a farrier leading a team of mules into the smithy. He trotted over to the sweaty man and waited until the team drank from the water trough.

"I just got back. Can you tell me what that's about?" Allen pointed to the lowered flags.

The farrier shook his head sadly. "It's the president, lad. 'e was assassinated, he was, on the 14th. Sad business it is, for the 'ole country."

Allen, stunned, thanked the blacksmith. He trudged away several yards, where he sank on the lowest rung of the board fence of the corral. He needed a little time to think and pull himself together. It hardly seemed possible such a thing could be, after four long years of war. How could it have happened and why? What would happen now?

When three quarters of an hour had passed, Allen stirred. There was little he could do but see to his own future; the country's future was out of his hands. Taking a deep breath, he set his course for the White House.

*   *   *

Lucy heard the *clump, clump* of boots before she saw the soldier. A wave of irritation welled up within her. She had just scrubbed the floors and it was off limits to the soldiers. Of course some errant officer had probably forgotten some personal effect, but she had put the items she found in a box on the porch. Not only were the soldiers forgetful, they were blind as well.

Tromp, clump, tromp. Lucy stayed her ground, on the top-most step and waited. *Add slow to that list,* she mentally intoned.

The soldier appeared, a private no less. Lucy knew Cook Sammy had worn off on her when sharp words were ready to surface. Dusty boots on her clean floors! She opened her mouth, "Private, you're not supposed to be–"

He took off his hat and looked up at her. The clock, in the sitting room, ticked heavy in the silence, convincing them time had not actually stopped.

"—*alive?*" Lucy asked. Could it be true that the soldier standing there, as dazed and surprised as her, was Allen? Lucy was glad her heart was young and faithful or she felt as if she might let go of life.

"Lucy." He smiled. "You're still here."

162

"Where else would I be?" Her voice was nearly a whisper. He mounted a step, then trundled up two more, and paused. "You didn't expect me to come back or what?"

She shook her head, realizing she still wore her dusting head kerchief. She snatched it off. "No. I mean you were missing in action, and I was sure–after all this time–you were, well, not coming back."

"I guess this is a surprise then." He took up another step.

"More than that, I think." She brushed off her dress and descended, relief giving way to nervousness.

"And you missed me?" he inquired, wadding up his hat in his hands in apprehension.

"I thought you were dead." Lucy warned herself not to cry, not now when she was standing only a few feet from the very live man.

Allen stood below her until only one step separated them. "You cared that I was dead?"

"Cared? Well, you could say that, except with a lot more emphasis." She studied his face as she soaked up the warmth in his eyes.

"Then you remember your promise?" he asked.

"Is that all you remember?" she pressed back.

"No. I seem to remember a lot more than that."

"Like?"

"Let's see. Like about maybe you taking on a little longer name."

"I hoped you would remember that." She laughed prettily.

"And you? Do you remember another promise?" he quizzed.

"Something about if you won the war?"

"Which I did," he grinned.

"And if you don't get yourself killed?" she finished.

"Which I didn't."

"I thought you did," she said softly.

"But I didn't. I'm here now," he spoke gently.

Lucy drew a deep breath and gave him a tremulous smile, fully aware of the one step separating them. "I seem to have forgotten. You'll have to refresh my memory."

Allen rose to the challenge, and then suddenly hesitated. "You do remember, right?"

Her eyes danced with merriment, "Well–." She gave a mischievous smile. Allen cut it off and redeemed his promise. The gap in the stairway disappeared.

*   *   *

The sweet smell of lilacs was borne on the mild air, wafting through the opened vertical windows of the church. Their scent contained the mystery of all that was good to Lucy— enduring life and love.

Lucy sat on the wooden bench in the simple church, nestled between Mama and Narciss. It would be the last time they sheltered her as such. Many of the friends she had at Camp Nelson had assembled as well: Naomi and Ruby, Captain Hall, Cook Sam and Sergeant Ribford. The Reverends Schofield and Burdett were in attendance. Rev. Fee and his family were present and to Lucy's joy, Burritt had come. There was Allen, resplendent in his blue uniform that had been freshly laundered.

A nervous smile adorned his face, along with a thin sheen of perspiration on his upper lip. He sat in the front pew, on the right, and gazed at Lucy, seated in the left wing. The couple shared shy expectant smiles and rightly so. Today was their wedding day, in the little church built by those freedmen who remained on the grounds of nearby Camp Nelson.

Reverend Gabriel Burdett rose before the group assembled. He had once been a slave but had become a minister and followed his desire as a soldier. He listened now for a moment to the birdsong that flitted in the air before he spoke.

"We have gathered today to witness the union of this man and this woman." He looked to Lucy and Allen, where they were seated. "This will be a union made by free choice, no one has forced these two people into this marriage. This is just one of the wonders we are going to witness. There will be no more 'jumping over the broom' marriages for us. And I say Amen

164

to that."

He continued, after smiling at the congregation. "There will be more choices ahead, dear ones, many, many more. We're going to have to rise to this challenge. We are going to have to make choices like the freed people we are, educated and productive ones.

"We've come into the Jubilee–our time–just as the Israelites did. We've come out of the wilderness. But in time, the Israelites fell away from the true God. Let that be an example to us. Let us not fall away. We have a challenge before us, which we have the fortitude to conquer. We have survived slavery, and we're ready for whatever the future holds, for whatever choices that have to be made to live in this land. We must choose the right ones, the right way, regardless of wrongs. We all know there will be more wrongs, given man's nature, but we will rise above them. It tells us in the 107th Psalm, 'And he led them forth by the right way'. God is our Guide! Amen to that!

"Now folks, we'll let Rev. Fee join the hands and hearts of these two dear young people, and we'll all feel the glory of it too."

He sat down and Rev. Fee rose, addressing the congregation. "I think we can all say a hearty yea and amen to Brother Burdett's words." He motioned for Lucy and Allen to stand before him. Lucy did, not in a rustle of white or even dreamy green silk, but in a dress of navy blue. Ever practical, Mama had secured the material exclaiming over its "serviceable" quality. Lucy, in her blissful state, would have accepted a gunnysack.

Rev. Fee began, "Dearly beloved, we are gathered together today in the presence of the Lord. We can be assured that He is here to witness this joyous occasion with us, because He tells us, 'Where two or three are gathered together in my name, there am I in the midst of them.' I am sure that He is smiling as He surveys this happy couple that have found each other and desire to be joined today in holy matrimony. Now I don't believe in too many words before we solemnize this marriage, but I would like to read that little story of love in the Garden of Eden."

There was a short pause as Rev. Fee rustled the pages of his Bible. Lucy's eyes had taken on a shining quality. "Ah, here: 'And the Lord God said, It is not good that the man should be alone; I will make him an help meet for him. And the Lord God caused a deep sleep to fall upon Adam, and he slept: and he took one of his ribs, and closed up the flesh instead thereof; And the rib, which the Lord God had taken from man, made he a woman, and brought her unto the man. And Adam said, This is now bone of my bones, and flesh of my flesh: she shall be called Woman, because she was taken out of Man. Therefore shall a man leave his father and mother and shall cleave unto his wife: and they shall be one flesh.' Now dear ones, isn't that a beautiful story? We see how man and woman were made for each other and brought together; we rejoice today with this dear couple that they also desire to be one flesh.

"Now, marriage is honorable in all and was instituted by an all-wise Creator. It should be entered into with reverence and true reflection as nothing but death can release you.

"Allen Ross, do you agree to take Lucy to be your lawful and wedded wife, and to love, cherish, nourish, and maintain her in sickness and in health, and to forsake all others, until it please God to separate you by death?"

Allen's deep "I do" filled the farthest corners of the room.

"And do you, Lucy, agree to take Allen Ross to be your lawful and wedded husband, and to love, cherish, nourish, and assist him in sickness and in health, and to forsake all others, until it please God to separate you by death?"

With only two small words I gain a last name. And a lifetime of love. Lucy's words radiated sunshine. "I do."

Rev. Fee's eyes sparkled at the couple. "You may join right hands." Placing his hand over theirs, he intoned, "What therefore God hath joined together, let not man put asunder. By virtue and authority of this license I hold, I pronounce you husband and wife."

In a short order of time, without pageantry or drama, with loved ones present to witness, Lucy and Allen made their vows before God. Rev. Fee turned the couple to face the congregation. "I announce to you, Mr. and Mrs. Allen Ross." There was a moment of silence, and then whistles started, followed by much fanfare.

Soon the jubilant shouts and whistling came to a halt, and Rev. Fee was joined by Rev. Burdett, who spoke.

"Church, we've got a long haul ahead of us, but WE ARE FREE! Free to raise our children where things are good. We all have a job to do before we get to our eternal home, but like this young couple before us, the road ahead looks mighty good. Mighty good! Now, in closing, someone start a hymn."

A deep baritone filled the clapboard church. Simultaneously, more voices joined in until the church's very frame seemed to vibrate as even the whitewash warmed to the tune. The birds stilled as they listened from the pine and honey locust:

Get right church and let's go home,
You better get right church and let's go home,
Get right church, Oh–get right church,
Get right church and let's go home.

I'm goin' home on the morning train,
I'm goin' home on the morning train,
I'm goin' home, Oh–I'm goin' home,
I'm goin' home on the morning train.

Evening train might be too late,
Evening train might be too late,
Evening train, Oh–that evening train,
Evening train might be too late.

Get right church and let's go home,
You better get right church and let's go home,
Get right church, Oh–get right church,
Get right church and let's go home.

The last refrain receded and gently dissipated like a mist lifting off a dewy meadow. There was a joyful hope in those present as many linked arms and clasped hands. Indelibly molded by the war, they were forever comrades.

At the top of the steps leading out of the church, Lucy and Allen paused in contentment. Unmindful of the throng, Allen turned to his bride. "Remember the last time we stood on a stairway?" He was grinning.

"Yes. There was a fulfillment of a promise." Lucy couldn't contain the smile that wreathed her face.

Allen lifted his eyes to the cerulean sky reflecting only brilliant sunshine. Then Lucy and Allen walked right out of the church and stepped freely into a new life.

1920

Epilogue

"So there now, you know all 'bout it. Powerful lot of livin' packed in those early years. Powerful lot more that followed." Mammy clutched her worn housedress to her, feeling the fabric with ungainly fingers. Her mind wanted to play tricks on her. It would have her see faded cotton shadowed by dim barn light. She forced her eyes past the cobwebs of yesterday to the present.

She was seated in her rocker with her two granddaughters before her. Time sprung to its correct existence. "Why you girls so quiet? Say something!"

Esther and Ethel exchanged looks. Esther spoke, "We don't know what to say, Mammy. Your story's–well–it's surprised us."

Mammy narrowed her eyes. "Huh. You thought old people popped up like mushrooms under a log? They've lived lives–that's how they got to be old." Now Mammy softened. She reached out a gnarled hand. The girls took it. "You girls are makin' your own stories."

Ethel folded her hands in her lap. "They won't be nothing like yours, Mammy."

"Be thankful. My story has got more sorrow in it than you know, girls." She clutched her housedress to her. "You go on now and finish what you started."

The two sisters worked in silence, their minds full of Mammy's story. When their ministrations were completed, Esther wrapped a blanket around her grandmother.

Esther knelt down and smiled at the old woman. "You've got more to tell us, Mammy? More we can learn from?"

Mammy thought for a moment. "There's more to tell, more to learn too. But …." Old Lucy halted. She felt strange like as if maybe time had double-crossed her. As if the timeline of her life wanted to shorten itself until she knew only seventeen summers again. She revisited a flowing menagerie of people she once knew. Suddenly she felt connected to ol' Cissie and Jambrel–their images reflected clearly before her mind's eye. In her memories, Mama and Rev. Fee were etched vividly, followed by Miss Fair. How much wisdom these beings had imparted to a young Lucy! Their words had given guidance and had a hand in her destiny.

Old Lucy's flashbacks brought her faithfully home to the rocker and her granddaughters, whose dark eyes regarded her solemnly. And in a moment of complete clarity, Lucy knew what her aged stiff bones could still do, what the sands of time within her hourglass of a memory could give to her offspring. She had no means to provide for the girls' comfort or provisions to enable them to be materially independent, but she did have wisdom–that pearl of great price–hard won only by living. She would share more with them … but not today. Today she was tired, her age limiting her like some sort of master. She fussed about, assuring herself her buttons were closed, that the blanket covered her feet.

When she was too worn for that, she looked wearily at Ethel and Esther. "You can hear more another day. Get me to my bed." The girls complied.

As she rose laboriously, Lucy looked around for a straw pallet on the floor but there was none. Neither was there a cot with a scratchy wool blanket. Instead there stood a feather bed with clean white sheets. Lucy's exclamation was soft, full of pleasure. She burrowed down within the bed, paying no mind to her granddaughters. She was so close to the end–the final chapter of her life. The warbling song of her flesh now bordered the great symphony where her soul would become conductor. Lucy knew all this because of her gained wisdom. Yes, she would give a gift of it to her granddaughters. Not today, but perhaps tomorrow. Yes, tomorrow, before the Good Shepherd called her home–to the Great House amid the clouds.

Afterword

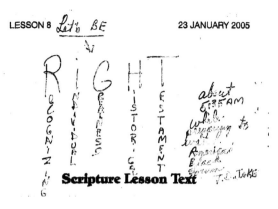

Scripture Lesson Text

In the early morning of the 23rd of January 2005, I experienced an epiphany-like event while preparing for my Sunday school lesson that morning. In a flash the word RIGHT was given to me and in the same sudden instance the acronym Recognizing Individual Greatness in Historical Testament came to me. The title of the lesson that morning was instructive, "Jesus Called for Total Commitment".* Even if I didn't know yet how to apply the divinely inspired message in a meaningful way in my daily walk, my mind was flooded with thoughts of Let's Be RIGHT—Let's Get RIGHT (with God) and Let's Do the RIGHT thing.

The following week's lesson seemed to be validating and confirming to me because it was entitled "Jesus Defined True Greatness".* I'm no theologian so I realize that my interpretation and utilization of this message will be scrutinized. Some will say that my outlook is an apple and oranges approach and that I am conflating a spiritual and religious message and attaching to it a secular and political application. Perhaps, but my ultimate purpose is to create a dialogue about whose standard for greatness we should embrace.

The RIGHT Concept, which follows, evolved from this transforming occurrence and became the basis for my beliefs relating to the issues of "naming rights" and diversity initiatives.

Lucy's Story: Right Choices But Wrongs Still Left is a continuance of what I hope to promote as a public dialogue in acknowledging the past and being proactively inclusive in our future.

Larry Hamilton

* *Bible Expositor and Illustrator* (Cleveland: Union Gospel Press, 2005)

RIG_{in}HT

Recognizing

Individual

Greatness

Historical

Testament

This concept embodies the concern over the historical bias in naming patterns and the contemporary artificial barriers limiting the expansion of ownership identity to public properties, and thus further imposing limitations upon those individuals belonging to groups that had traditionally been denied consideration. RIGHT seeks to re-evaluate the standards of heroism and societal acceptance of those who may have been deemed not to be valued or worthy of having their names adorn public facilities. RIGHT advocates a proactive effort in naming public properties that is more reflective of the diversity within the community and that acknowledges from a historical perspective the merit of greater inclusion with regards to race, gender, ethnic and national origin in expanding ownership identity.

RIG_{in}HT

Recognizing
Individual
Greatness
Historical
Testament

Mission statement
RIGHT promotes the development of community partnerships in naming public properties that is more reflective of diversity. Honoring and memorializing the service of people historically excluded from ownership identity should merit greater inclusion in the process of naming public property.

Vision statement
Making vision reality through promoting equality of opportunity in the naming process of public property.

Belief statements
We believe that the Gospel commandment to "love others as we love ourselves" is the key to living the Christian life and showing ourselves as Children of the Light.

We believe that streets or municipal facilities can be named without regard to residency requirements or other such artificial barriers.

We believe in permitting dual name designation of streets but in allowing for the original street name for mailing or postal consideration to be retained.

We believe that the purchase or sale of municipal property with ownership identity implications or the annexation of land to the city be discussed as relates to the *RIGHT* concept.

We believe that the sale of ownership identity within facilities and or the commercialization of public properties be monitored and the RIGHT concept discussed or noted prior to sale.

Larry Hamilton, a native of Loveland, Ohio, is a retired teacher of African American History, World Studies and Current Events who resides in Piqua, Ohio.

Hamilton graduated cum laude with a B.S. in Education/History & Political Science in 1971 from Central State University where he was a member of Phi Alpha Theta History Honor Society and Alpha Kappa Mu National Honor Society as well as President of Delta Xi Chapter of Alpha Phi Alpha Fraternity.

He earned a master's degree in education from Wright State University in 1979 and has taken additional course offerings at Edison Community College and the University of Dayton.

He is a founding member of the African American Genealogy Group of the Miami Valley (AAGGMV), has authored an article, "Helping African Ancestored Americans Find Their Roots," and is a frequent presenter on family history and genealogy. In August of 2005, he appeared as a genealogy researcher in the episode, "The Slave Banjo," on PBS-TV's The History Detectives.

In addition, Hamilton invented the educational game, NEWS OR LOSE, developed and conducted the Ohio Scholars Bowl Competition, founded the non-profit organization Promoting Recognition of Diversity (PROD) to recruit minority candidates to teach in Piqua City Schools and developed the RIGHT concept to promote community partnerships for naming public properties.

Hamilton was selected for Who's Who Among America's Teachers. He was awarded the Ohio Tri-County NAACP's Martin Luther King Outstanding African American Award and received the state of Ohio's MLK Cultural Awareness Award in 2005.